I0787975

SKY RIDER

BOOK 3

CRAIG HALLORAN

Dragon Wars: Sky Rider - Book 3

By Craig Halloran

★ ★ ★ ★

Copyright © 2019 by Craig Halloran

Amazon Edition

TWO-TEN BOOK PRESS

PO Box 4215, Charleston, WV 25364

ISBN eBook: 978-1-946218-70-4

ISBN Paperback: 978-1-654613-31-0

ISBN Hardback: 978-1-946218-71-1

www.craighalloran.com

Publisher's Note

This book is a work of fiction. Names, characters, places, and incidents either are the product of the author's imagination or are used fictitiously, and any resemblance to actual persons, living or dead, events, or locales is entirely coincidental.

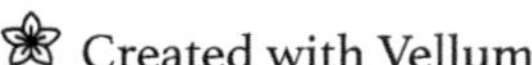 Created with Vellum

THE LANDS OF GAPOLI
ICE VALE
DARK MOUNTAIN
FKIRSTICK
UGRAD
GREEN RIDGE
BLACK MOSS
CREEK SCOWL
LOOSE BOOT
KENNA
DAGGER FORD
WESTERLUND
PORTAM
HARBOR LAKE
ARROWWOOD
MONARCH CITY
WILLOWACKS
RAVEN CLIFF
HILLS
RED BONE
RAVENSTOCK
FARNOOK
SULTAR SLAY
VALLEY
SHIRE
SALT KNOB
OLDHAM
PEBBLE BOLT
GUNDER ISLAND
GOLD HOOK
CROW VALLEY
LAKE FLUGEN
THE SHELF
LITTLETON
DWARF SKULL

1

"Anya! Anya!" Grey Cloak screamed at the top of his lungs, struggling against the iron grip of Cinder the dragon's talons. "Take me back! You have to take me back!"

Cinder's black wings flapped in a powerful motion that lifted them higher into the stormy sky. The swirling winds must have drowned out Grey Cloak's voice, because if Anya heard him, she didn't acknowledge it.

He craned his neck, trying to find Anya the Sky Rider and make eye contact, and continued yelling. "Anya! You have no right to do this! No right at all! Zooks!"

If Grey Cloak could have shaken his fist at Anya, he would have. But he wasn't going anywhere. Cinder was holding him fast like a hawk that had snatched a bass out of the water. The dragon's talons were stronger than iron bands wrapped around his body. Grey Cloak squirmed and twisted, but his effort was futile.

They were soaring through the blackness of the night sky, and the wind was tearing through his jet-black hair. As the dragon flew into the clouds, the ground fell away, and Grey Cloak couldn't see anything. His heart raced. *How far up am I, anyway?*

Grey Cloak had been around dragons ever since he could remember, but he'd never ridden any of them. The experience was as euphoric as it was terrifying. At any moment, Cinder could drop him, and he would plummet helplessly to his death. He swallowed a cold lump in his throat.

"Anya?"

He didn't like feeling helpless or being at the mercy of others. That was one of the main causes of why he'd fled from Dark Mountain. No one was going to tell him what to do or how to live his life. That made him angry. And Anya had snatched him away without his consent. His temper began to boil. "Anya!"

Thunder rumbled loudly, and flashes of lightning lit up the clouds. He caught a glimpse of Anya's leg above him and screamed again, "Anya, let me down!"

Cinder cut through the clouds, unfettered by the storm and the rain. His wings beat harder and faster.

The skin of Grey Cloak's cheeks flapped. "What's the hurry?" he hollered.

The dragon dipped and rose then barrel-rolled and dove.

Grey Cloak's stomach turned inside out. *"Ulp."*

The longer they flew, the madder he became as more guilt rose inside him. He'd been ripped away from the only friends he had left—Rhonna, Lythlenion, and Tanlin. They were in pursuit of Zora, a half-elf thief, who'd been kidnapped by the Scourge, a band of adventurers led by a man named Sash. The fish-eyed warrior meant business. He'd taken them all down in Daggerford, and it was Grey Cloak's fault.

But that was only the beginning of Grey Cloak's problems. They were supposed to be rescuing his blood brother, Dyphestive. He had been taken by the Doom Riders, who were led by a wicked woman named Drysis the Dreadful. Grey Cloak had blindly rushed after his brother, back into the teeth of danger, with no sort of plan.

And it showed. Everything he'd tried had failed, and Anya was taking him in the opposite direction of where he wanted to be. At least, he thought it was the opposite. The truth was that he didn't have any idea where he was going.

"Anya!" he tried to shout above the storm. Thunder boomed like an angry god. He yelled louder. "Anya!"

The howling wind in his ears was his answer.

Cinder's talons clenched. *Quit crying like a baby. It's obvious that she can't hear you. But once I'm down on the ground, we are going to have a talk.*

"Ow! What are you doing? Squeezing the juice out of me?" He bared his teeth and bit Cinder's talon. "*Blech!* That tastes awful." He spit. "What a stupid thing to do."

Through the thick clouds, he caught glimpses of Cinder's body as it drifted left and right. A long tail like a cedar waved behind the amazing beast. With his eyes following the tail of the dragon, Grey Cloak tried to get his bearings. *He needs to get out of these clouds. I need to see something.*

Beyond Cinder's tail, something else was flying through the inky darkness. A burning ball of green flashed through the mist and vanished again.

"Uh, Cinder, did you see that?" Grey Cloak asked in a voice that was inaudible over the wind. He narrowed his eyes. Something cut through the clouds behind them. It looked like it had eyes like burning balls of emerald green. He blinked. *I must be seeing things. With all of those lightning flashes, one never knows what they might hallucinate.*

Two bodies crisscrossed behind them only a few yards from the very end of Cinder's tail.

Grey Cloak stretched his neck. *Now I know I saw that. What in the world could be up here?*

The flying bodies surged forward. They were winged creatures covered in scales, with claws for hands on the tips of their wings. Their burning gaze bored into Grey Cloak.

"Drakes!" he yelled. "Drakes!"

Drakes were dragons but not full-bloods like Cinder. They were pony-sized lizards that didn't have full front legs like dragons.

Cinder made a hard turn that threw Grey Cloak's stomach into his chest. He lost sight of the drakes. As Cinder snaked a wild path through the air, the drakes reappeared. The long necks of the three beasts stretched out and rattled like snake tails. The drakes let out hungry shrieks and snapped and bit at Cinder's tail.

"Go away!" Grey Cloak said futilely. He knew all about the drakes from his time in Dark Mountain. He'd never cared for them, not one bit. They were wild dragons that thrived in hovels of their own, but they served the cause of Black Frost. All of them were known to be vicious hunters. Only death could stop them from bringing down their prey. *Not good. Not good at all!*

With his arms fastened to his sides, Grey Cloak could do nothing but watch the slavering horrors with razor-sharp teeth and claws close in. He tossed his head back and yelled as loudly as he could, "Anya, we have company!"

As if his words had been heard, Cinder thrust straight up into the sky above a blanket of murky clouds, revealing the stunning sight of a star-filled sky burning bright on a tapestry of black.

Cinder slowed his ascent. With his wings beating gently, he stood upright, hovering in the air. Five drakes burst out of the carpet of clouds and surrounded him, and Grey Cloak's breath caught as Cinder let out a deafening roar.

The drakes shrieked in hungry delight and attacked.

2

What was left of Talon was standing underneath the rocky ledges of the Dark Ridges with the rain pouring down all around them. Rhonna was pacing underneath the nook in the rocks, muttering. The dwarven blacksmith had seen better days.

Lythlenion, the half-orc cleric, was squatting against the wall, rocking back and forth and humming. Tanlin had wrapped his narrow body in a traveling cloak, his teeth chattering, and was wringing his hands. The older man had a nervous look in his eyes, and he acted like he was about to say something but didn't. The group had been stupefied since Grey Cloak was snatched away less than an hour ago.

No one had said a word until Lythlenion broke the silence. "Why don't I make a fire?"

"Forget it," Rhonna said. "There's no telling what other terrors might crawl out of these hills at night. I'm not taking any more chances. Not after what happened with Grey Cloak and that dragon. Oy! I haven't been on the bad side of fortune in a long time."

"I would like a fire," Tanlin said bitterly, nearly drowned out by the heavy rain. "Nothing else is going to crawl out of these black hills. Not on a night like this. Besides..." He shivered. "I'm freezing."

"No," Rhonna said.

"I beg your pardon, but I don't seem to recall anyone placing you in charge," Tanlin said.

"No, but I'm in charge of him." She pointed her lantern-shaped jaw at Lythlenion. "And he would be the one making the fire."

"Well, you aren't *in charge*," Lythlenion said politely. "I volunteered my services because you asked me. But I agree, we shouldn't make a fire. Too many creatures will seek shelter and warmth from the cold." He opened a small leather pouch and produced a handful of nuts. "Try these, Tanlin. They will warm you up."

Tanlin shuffled over to the half-orc and stretched out his hand. "What are they?"

"Fire kernels. They stoke the fires within," Lythlenion said.

"Never heard of them, and right now, I'll try anything."

Tanlin took the nuts and started eating. "Oh my, that's spicy."

Lythlenion offered him a waterskin. "You would do well to wash them down."

Tanlin drank and let out a relief-filled "Ahhh!" He wiped his sleeve across his mouth and sighed. "I'm sorry if I sound soft. It's to my shame, as I've been on my fair share of adventures. And in much harder conditions than this. But the men and women that I traveled with spoiled me. They handled much of the watch." He shivered again. "And for some reason, I feel out of my element."

"You should. You're on the edge of Ugrad," Rhonna said. "Have you been this far north before?"

"No," Tanlin replied. He wiggled his eyebrows. "Well now, I think those fire kernels are working." He gave Lythlenion an approving nod. "I thank you. Now for the matter at hand. What are we going to do, and who is going to lead?"

"Huh!" Rhonna said.

"I meant no offense, but we have to have a leader between us. Since I'm a member of Talon and the only one left, then I'm the ranking member. And even though I haven't led many expeditions of this sort, I feel well qualified to pursue Zora."

Rhonna marched over to Tanlin and poked her thick finger in his chest. "Listen, bub. We aren't members of Talon.

We are members of me and him." She pointed at Lythlenion. "But in order to simplify matters, I say we put it to a vote. I vote for me, you vote for you. Lythlenion, who do you vote for?"

Lythlenion looked between the two of them then stood up and said, "Me."

"Ah geesh, you can't vote for yourself too!" Rhonna said. "And you've never led anything."

"Well, I have too. You haven't been around for all of my exploits. Besides, I'm older and bigger than the both of you."

"What's that supposed to mean?" Rhonna asked.

"I don't know. I just don't want to see people arguing. I wish Grey Cloak were still here to lead us."

Rhonna tilted her head to one side. "What are you talking about?" She thumbed her chest. "He wasn't leading us. I was."

"Oh. Well, I was of the distinct impression that I was following Grey Cloak. I assumed everyone was," Lythlenion said.

"I was following Grey Cloak too," Tanlin added. "And I'm not sure why, but it seemed natural."

"He's a stripling," Rhonna said.

"Ha-ha," Lythlenion said. He patted Rhonna's shoulder. "Just pulling your beard."

"He is more than a stripling, though," Tanlin added. "Why else would a Sky Rider have snatched him?" He combed his hair back with his fingers. "Rhonna, I'm not going to fight with you. As long as you are dedicated to finding Zora, I'll follow you. But I hope that you'll honor my input."

Rhonna fastened her hand on Tanlin's forearm and said, "I swear on the beard of my father that we will make every effort to get Zora back."

Tanlin nodded. "I can live with that. The truth is, if we can catch up to the Scourge, we stand a good chance of slipping away with Zora. She's very capable of escaping, and once she has a window, she'll take it. We need only to be in the vicinity to scoop her up."

Rhonna nodded. "The problem is catching up. We can't do it on foot. We only have one horse, and we can't all ride it or keep up. But if we leave now, it's possible that we might catch them napping. What do you say?"

"As long as those fire kernels hold up, I'm up for moving. Perhaps my thin skin will toughen up along the way," Tanlin said.

Lythlenion nodded. "There's nothing quite like a long walk in the rain."

"Good. I'll get the horse." She plodded out from underneath the dry pocket in the rocks. Her hardened gaze searched the darkness, but she found no sign of the horse anywhere. "Well, kiss my anvil. I think that dragon spooked our horse. It's probably a league away by now."

"What do we do?" Lythlenion said.

"It had what is left of our gear. We go after it."

Rhonna led the small company through the Dark Ridges, but they didn't make it five hundred yards before they were surrounded by spear-wielding lizard men that had been lurking in the rocks.

As she eyed her scaly foes, Rhonna cursed, "Horseshoes!"

3

nya stood up in the stirrups of Cinder's saddle and surveyed her enemies. Five drakes were surrounding them after having followed them since shortly after they lifted off of the ground, much to the thanks of Grey Cloak's screaming. The fearsome lizards' green eyes glared at them.

Cinder let out a furious roar that overtook the rumbling thunder. Heat rose underneath Anya's saddle as fire unleashed from his throat. A torrent of flames engulfed a drake, which flew straight into Cinder's jaws of death.

Anya slid a javelin out of her oversized quiver, and its wood turned bright white. "Summon the thunder!" she cried. She hurled it toward an oncoming drake. The thunder javelin soared straight and true, transforming into a bolt of lightning and ripping through the drake's gaping maw before shooting out of its back. *Two down. Three to go.*

A drake pinned itself on the back of Cinder's wings. The huge dragon let out an angry roar then bit down on the drake's wings and ripped them off, flinging flesh and scales from its body. The drake plummeted in a clumsy spiral and vanished in the clouds. Cinder spit its wings out.

The nape of Anya's neck tingled, and she twisted around right before a drake dropped out of the sky and sank its claws into her shoulders. "*Ugh!*"

The drake's wings beat fiercely as it tried to rip her out of the saddle, but she kept her toes hooked in the stirrups. With a twist of the wrist, she pulled her sword—a shimmering blade with dragon-wing pommels—out of its sheath.

Though the drake struck at Anya like a snake, she jammed the tip of her sword through its stubby jaw and snout. Its talons unlocked from her shoulders. Like an angry bird, it hovered in the air, mercilessly attacking.

Anya twisted her hips into her next lethal swing. The razor-sharp edge of her sword cut clean though the drake's serpentine neck. Its body went one way, and the head and neck fell the other into the clouds, which swallowed them.

The last drake let out fearful shriek, and Cinder spit a stream of fire at it. The drake slipped underneath the fire and vanished in the clouds.

As she pulled another javelin from the sheath, Anya said, "Cinder, go after it! It will alert the others."

Cinder sank into the clouds like a great whale diving into the sea. His tremendous wings flapped faster, and he accelerated through the sky.

Anya narrowed her eyes. The drakes were very fast dragons and extremely agile in the air. But so was Cinder. It was an aerial version of cat and mouse. She caught fleeting glimpses of the drake snaking through the clouds, veering left and right before vanishing again. She cocked her javelin back and stood tall with her feet locked in the stirrups. "Catch him!"

"It's not as easy as it looks," Cinder said. "I would like to see you chase down a chicken and catch it with your bare hands."

"If you don't catch him, we're going to have a lot more than him to worry about! He's heading north!"

"I'm well aware."

"I only need a good look! Just one!"

Cinder's body rolled left and right. Anya swayed above the saddle, knees bouncing, but held fast. With her auburn hair flapping from underneath her helmet, she locked her sight on the tail of the drake. She launched the thunder javelin.

The missile whistled through the air and transformed into a bolt of lightning. The drake vanished in the clouds, and so did the javelin. A moment later, a bright flash lit up the clouds, followed by the muffled sound of something exploding.

Cinder flew into a cloud that was peppered with scattered scales. He dropped underneath the cloud bank just in time to see parts of the drake plummeting toward the ground. "Well done, young lady," he said with a nod of approval. "Well done."

Anya dropped into her saddle and patted Cinder on the neck. "Take us down. Somewhere dry. Let's see how our passenger is doing."

He glided back down to earth and landed in a grove of shrubbery in the plains then gently let Grey Cloak slide out of his grip. The ashen elf stumbled through the knee-high grass, dropped to his knees, clutched his belly, and started yacking.

"Apparently, someone doesn't like my flying," Cinder said.

Anya smiled as Grey Cloak gathered his feet underneath him and wiped his mouth on his sleeve.

"What's with all of that flying around and treating me like a salt shaker? I feel green."

"You *look* green," she said. "And we wouldn't have had to do that if you hadn't howled like a baby wolf."

"You're blaming me?" He jabbed his fingers against his chest. "You kidnapped me! Rotten cherries, I'm going to puke again." He dashed away, hid among the thatches, and hurled.

4

The lizard men had Rhonna, Lythlenion, and Tanlin outnumbered eight to three. They were a tall and muscular bunch, with lizard faces and snakelike scales for skin. Unlike lizards, they wore clothes like men—buckskin and leather jerkins—and didn't have tails. Their brawny shoulders gave them a neckless appearance. Aside from their different dress and assortment of weapons, which they carried or wore on their hips, one didn't look much different from the other. Judging by the looks of them, Rhonna thought were wild brigands. But worst of all, they were flesh eaters too.

"What do we have here?" one of the lizard men asked. He stood out from the rest of the bunch. The others' skin had an olive-green tone, but his face and skin were a rich bloodred. His slender tongue would flick out of his mouth, and he had a hiss in his voice when he spoke. "Are you lost? This is a dangerous place to be lost."

Rhonna took a quick head count of the of the lizard men. She counted eight initially, but a couple more were hidden in the shadows. They had horses, too, but most importantly, they had her company's horse. One of the lizard men was holding it by the bit and bridle. "We aren't lost, but our horse is," she said gruffly. She set her eyes on the chestnut-brown mare they'd bought in Daggerford. "I see you found it. I thank you. We'll take our horse and be moving on."

The heavy rain suddenly subsided to a misty drizzle. The leader stepped into her path and said, "Not so fast, dwarfie." He glowered down at her, his bright-yellow eyes burning with sinister intent. "How do we know that this is your horse? It looks like our horse to me."

She glared up at him and said, "Listen, reptile—"

"It's Jondark," the lizard man corrected.

The other lizard men made angry hisses.

Jondark waggled his finger—showing a sharp nail that could scale a fish—in her face and said, "Don't insult me or my brood. We are not reptiles. We are peoples, the same as you."

"You aren't the same as me. Trust me. We aren't a bunch of low-life horse thieves," she said.

The angry hisses of the surrounding lizard men grew louder. Jondark's brow knitted. "You are impudent!"

"And you are ignorant. Do you really think that it is just the three of us?" She stepped toward him until her chest touched the tip of his spear. "Do you?"

Jondark's eyes slid from side to side. His brood's necks began to twist.

Rhonna laid it on thick. "That's not *our* horse. We were merely sent to fetch it. That is one of Oluf Rieschman Gwunderstaff's mares. That's right. *The* Oluf Rieschman Gwunderstaff! One of the greatest generals of Monarch City. We are merely his henchmen, doing his will, so that his precious soldiers, all ten squads of them, don't get their hands dirty. And that horse"—she stabbed her finger in the horse's direction—"is a gift for his niece. Yes, a gift that he bought from the breeder in Loose Boot."

The lizard men's leader had a nervous look in his eye. "We noticed no troops."

"Of course not, you idiot. They are in these hills, running drills. You aren't supposed to notice them." She peered over her shoulder and gazed at the ridges. "But they are out there, watching and waiting to strike. They are General Gwunderstaff's elite soldiers." Her voice became low and deadly. "The best."

"You are bluffing." He pushed her back with the tip of his spear. "No one knows the Dark Ridges better than Jondark's Brood. Ha! You are a lying little dwarf."

Tanlin cleared his throat and said, "Do what you want with us and the horse, but consider yourself warned.

General 'Bloodbath' Gwunderstaff will have no mercy on the fools who steal his horse and kill his servants. All of your brood will be wiped out. And he won't stop there. He'll wage war on all lizard people. He considers it practice."

"You take me for a fool. There is no General Gwunderstaff. And the only bloodbath is going to be yours."

Rhonna cast a nervous glance up at Lythlenion. He had a worried look in his eye. Her bluff failed. Perhaps Tanlin's had made it worse, and they were standing flat-footed inside a ring of spears.

"You see, we are hungry, and now that it has stopped raining, we can feast. On you!" Jondark stabbed his spear into the ground and lifted his arms high. In a mocking fashion, he said, "Mighty General Bloodbath Gwunderstaff! I call to you and your men! If you are out there, slay me where I stand!"

The only things that struck Jondark were the drizzling raindrops that slid down his scaly face.

Rhonna started to coil downward. She turned her head toward the lizard man she would fight first. All she could do was fight for her life. She eased her hand toward the dagger inside her cloak. *Bloody horseshoes, they're going to kill us all.*

Jondark began to lower his long arms. His triumphant smirk bared his fangs like a smiling crocodile. "Brethren, tonight we feast like kings. The meat of the orc and the dwarf will be tough, but this human offers succulent bones." He licked his thin lips with his lizard tongue. "Do you have any more lies you would like to share before you die, dwarfie?"

"When you are wandering through the fires of Hades, just remember that this little dwarfie warned you," Rhonna said. She'd coiled down just enough to spring. Lythlenion's breath became heavy behind her ear.

Jondark nodded as he eyed them all. "I see you want to fight. Hah. No dwarf is quicker than my brood's spears." He pulled his spear free from the ground and lifted it over his head, parallel to the ground. "Brothers, kill—"

5

Just as Rhonna was about to make her move, an arrow whistled overhead. *Thuk!*

Jondark's big body quavered. He had an arrow with black feathers stuck in the middle of his forehead. When he looked up at the missile, the spear fell from his fingertips and bounced off of his skull. He grabbed the arrow.

Behind Rhonna, Lythlenion caught his breath. The rest of the lizard men stood in gaping stupefaction.

Another arrow whistled through the air and lodged itself in Jondark's chest. *Thuk!* Jondark wobbled and fell.

The lizard men crouched with their serpentine heads moving on a swivel. *Thuk! Thuk!* Two more dropped to the ground under the powerful hail of black-feathered arrows.

Rhonna didn't waste another breath. The lizard men guarding her attacked. She grabbed one of their spears just above the tip as she pulled her dagger free. She stormed forward and plunged the blade into the lead lizard man's gut.

Lythlenion wrestled over a lizard man's spear. The two brutes tumbled over the ground.

Tanlin had disappeared.

Rhonna turned in time to catch a lizard man charging straight at her. She had no way to jump out of his path in time. He aimed his spear at her heart, his slanted eyes full of victory. She braced herself and stretched out her hands to try to stop the inevitable impact.

Thuk! The crescent-moon-shaped head of an arrow burst out of the front of the charging lizard man's chest.

Bowbreaker! "I told you fools that General Bloodbath was coming!" Rhonna chased after another lizard man. He chucked a spear at her, but she ducked, and the long missile missed. She jumped onto his chest, bore him to the ground, and killed him with her dagger.

Their small band had the lizard men on the run. They scattered like thieves with a lantern shining on them. But there was no avoiding the lethal terror that whistled through the night—the distinct sound that only Bowbreaker's arrows could make.

Thuk! A lizard man collapsed as he climbed into the saddle of his horse. An arrow was stuck in his temple.

Thuk! "Ack!" The last wide-eyed lizard man fell face-first with an arrow in the middle of his back.

Rhonna rose to her feet and scanned the area. All of the lizard men were on the ground. Lythlenion climbed over a lizard man and back to his feet, gasping.

Tanlin appeared out of nowhere. He was standing over a dead lizard man. "I killed this one," he said as he wiped his dagger on the dead lizard man's back. He pointed at the other lizard men. "But who killed all of them?"

"Bowbreaker," Rhonna said as her eyes searched the skyline.

"Who?" Tanlin asked.

She spied a figure walking along the nearby rocky ridges. He moved with the ease of a ghost. "Him."

Tanlin arched an eyebrow. "A friend of yours, I hope."

"Sometimes."

Bowbreaker jumped down the rocks and made his way down to ground level. He was tall for an elf and had jet-black hair parted in the middle. He wore a serious look on his face. His buckskin clothing fit him like a glove. His right arm, noticeably bigger than the other one, was sleeveless, and he was wearing bearskin boots. The only things he was carrying were a quiver full of arrows strapped behind his broad shoulders, a hunting knife, a small leather satchel, and the bow in his large hands, which was more than half as tall as he was.

"How long have you been following us?" Rhonna asked.

"I've been on your tail since the last time you saw me," Bowbreaker replied in a direct and impersonal manner. "It seemed like your situation had finally gotten out of hand."

"It's been out of hand since we were in Daggerford!" she said. "Where were you when a burning building was coming down all around us?"

"You know how I feel about cities," Bowbreaker said as he began pulling his arrows free of the dead bodies. He gestured to the arrow he was tugging free. "They go in easy, but they are difficult to get out. You have to twist them just right. I save the ones I can."

"Yes, he cherishes his arrows more than us," Rhonna replied.

"What are you so sour about? You're alive, aren't you?"

"I'm glad," Lythlenion said. He pushed his messy hair out of his eyes. "It's good to see you, old friend."

Bowbreaker nodded.

"Uh, allow me to introduce myself. I'm Tanlin, and I, too, am thankful for your timely services."

Rhonna ripped an arrow out of Jondark's chest. The moon-shaped arrowhead broke off at the tip. She tossed it at Bowbreaker and said, "Here is one of your precious arrows."

Bowbreaker picked up the arrow, which had bounced off his chest and fallen at his feet. He eyed the arrow's length. "The feathers are still good, and the shaft is still straight. I can fit a new head on it. Thank you, Rhonna."

She cleaned her dagger on a lizard man's trousers, slammed it into its sheath, and said, "I'm tired of you lingering around until you finally decide whether or not you want to get involved. Either you have our backs, or you don't."

"Precisely," Bowbreaker replied.

Rhonna make a choking motion with her hands and stormed forward.

Tanlin cut her off and said, "Bowbreaker is an interesting name. How did you come by that?"

Rhonna rolled her eyes. "Don't get him started."

Lythlenion took a knee and said, "I like that story, and I'm glad that you asked. Go ahead, Bowbreaker. Tell it."

Without cracking a smile, Bowbreaker held out his bow. It was made of black oak that was sanded down to a smooth-as-silk finish. At each end, tiny hands that appeared to be holding the bowstring were carved in the notches. The handle of the bow was made for a big hand, and the shaft was thicker than an ordinary bow. "As I was reaching manhood, I learned there wasn't a bow that I couldn't break. You see, I have very long arms, and when I stretched the string back along my cheek, to its full extension, the bow would break. The first time, I thought those ordinary elven bows were poorly made. But then, to the shock of my teachers, the bows broke again and again."

"Where were you taught?" Tanlin asked.

"In Arrowwood, of course. I come from a long line of

archers." He lifted a finger. "But the sages say that every so many generations, a great one is born. An elf with an arm so strong that he can fire the most powerful arrows. They call him Bowbreaker. And that is me."

Tanlin rubbed his chin and said, "It seems strange that you aren't serving your own kind. Certainly, the elves of Arrowwood, well, adore you."

"No. Quite the opposite. They fear me."

6

With the skies clearing, Grey Cloak shook the water from his gray garment. He took some deep breaths through his nose and allowed his tummy to settle.

"Are you feeling better?" Anya asked. She was standing in front of Cinder, who was lying in the grass. The mighty dragon's head was down on the ground, and his eyes were closed. "You are going to have a hard time learning to fly if you become queasy in the air."

"That's not a problem because I don't ever plan on flying again." He glanced upward. "Ever."

"Don't be silly. You are a *natural*. You have to learn to fly."

"Is that so?" He walked over the wet grass and faced her. "And why is that, exactly?"

"Because all naturals become Sky Riders or Riskers. That is how it is."

He shook his head. "Says who?"

She gave him a perplexed look.

"Let me guess," he continued. "You were taught that ever since you were a little girl? Right? You don't know any different."

"But we are the only ones that can ride the dragons. It is our gift. It is *your* gift."

Grey Cloak poked a finger at her and said, "The only gift that I want is freedom. You see, I've never had that. Ever since I can remember, I've been around naturals and dragons. They are all told who they are supposed to be. That they are so special. Well, guess what." He flapped his cloak. "I didn't like it. I just want to be me."

"But you can't. You are the son of Zanna Paydark, a legendary Sky Rider. You have to fulfill your destiny."

"Zanna Paydark?" He wiped the rain from his brow. "Is that my mother or my father?"

"It is a woman's name. Zanna. Everyone knows that." She frowned at him. "Zanna Paydark is your mother. It is a great honor."

He tightened his cloak around his shoulders. Grey Cloak had never known anything about his mother. He was an orphan, and even though he did wonder, he'd gotten used to not knowing. Hearing that his mother was a Sky Rider should have been thrilling, but instead, it sparked a fire in him. "If my mother was such a powerful Sky Rider, then tell me, what happened to her? Why did she abandon me?"

"Black Frost killed her. It is your destiny to avenge her and save the world from a darker fate."

Grey Cloak thought about it. "No, thanks."

"What?"

"If you can't hear me, then take that helmet off."

"I can hear you fine." Anya took her helmet off anyway. Her damp hair fell over her shoulders and clung to her rosy cheeks. She was stunning. "Grey Cloak, don't you want to avenge your mother? I want to avenge my parents. Black Frost killed them too. Every day, I burn inside, thinking about it."

"Well, every day, I've burned inside, thinking about nothing but freedom." He paced around her. "Listen, Sky Rider lady, did you ever stop to think that maybe, maybe, your parents would be alive if they hadn't taken on Black Frost in the first place? Haven't you ever heard, 'See no evil, speak no evil, hear no evil'? It's a pretty simple philosophy. Stay away from evil!"

Cinder huffed out a warm chuckle. With his eyes still closed, out of the corner of his mouth, he said, "He makes a valid point."

"Button it, Cinder!" She hooked Grey Cloak by the elbow as he circled her. "You don't know what you are talking about. Good men and women have died trying to keep the peace. If we don't stop Black Frost, the night will stay forever." She glared into his eyes. "It will be cold. As cold as death. And you won't have your precious freedom anymore."

He tried to pull away, but her strong grip held him fast. "I know that you can't know that. If you want to kill Black Frost, that's fine. But as for me, I have other plans in mind. And that would be living." He tried to peel her fingers away but couldn't. "Do you mind?"

She let go. "Why, you bitter little bridge troll!"

"Bridge troll? Me?"

"You heard me. Perhaps the Sky Riders are better off without the likes of you. You are self-centered. That is not a quality that we desire."

"Self-centered? Me?" He tapped his chest with his fingers. "Listen, Your Majesty, I was trying to rescue my friends, but you snatched me away. You tell me who is selfish. I have friends who need me. But instead, you want me to 'save the world.'" He made air quotes. "It's the stupidest thing I ever heard." He started marching north.

"Where do you think you are going? You are coming with me, whether you like it or not."

He turned and bowed to her. "No, I'm not, Your Majesty."

"Stop calling me that."

He saluted her. "Yes, Captain." When he backed away, he bumped into Cinder's tail. He tried to walk around the huge flexible appendage, but wherever he went, Cinder blocked him. He crouched low and jumped high. Wherever he went, Cinder's tail pushed him back like a cat toying with a mouse. He balled up his fists, jumped stiff legged, and stomped his feet. "Zooks!"

7

"We need to get going," Anya said as she put her helmet back on. "You'll have to save your temper tantrum for later. Cinder, scoop him up."

"No, wait! I don't want to fly again. I'm still queasy. And I can't leave my friends. I made a promise. Haven't you ever made a promise?"

"We aren't going north. Not with the drakes lurking in the Dark Ridges. It's too risky." She buckled the strap under her chin. "There are only a few of us Sky Riders left. Black Frost is determined to kill us all, unless he can turn us. And we are the only ones that can stop him. I'm sorry, but this is bigger than your companions. It's bigger than all of us."

Cinder rose. His huge paw scraped over the ground toward Grey Cloak.

Grey Cloak backed away. "Just because you take me

doesn't mean that I will do what you want. Do you really want a disgruntled elf to teach? I can be very annoying."

"You've made that clear," she said.

"Must you be so hardheaded?" He talked fast, trying to persuade her any way that he could. "Let's make a deal. Negotiate. I'll come willingly if you help me."

"No."

He stretched his arms out toward the dark northern horizon. "Come on. They can't be that far away. We have you and Cinder. The Scourge will be no match for us. Not only can we save Zora, but we can free a dragon too!"

"What dragon?" she asked.

"Uh, well, they said it was a crypt dragon, and it was about yea big." He measured out three feet between his hands. "Even during my time in the kennels of Dark Mountain, I never saw one like it. It had ivory scales and eyes that burned like pink roses."

Anya and Cinder exchanged serious glances.

"What?" He looked between the both of them. "You know this dragon, don't you?"

She marched over to him and lifted him to his toes by the collar. "You aren't making this up?"

He shrugged. "How could I make this up? It was there. It froze Zora with its stare. A wizard, Honzur, uses a dragon charm to control it."

Anya turned him around and pushed him in the back toward Cinder. "Get on."

"What? But I told you I'm still queasy."

"Do you want to save your friend or not?"

"Of course I do." He started climbing into Cinder's massive saddle. "But I find it very insulting that now you want to help to save a dragon, but you didn't want to save my friend. How convenient. You know what you are? You're a hypocrite."

She shoved him into the saddle. "And do you know what you are?"

"An elf?" he asked sarcastically.

"No, a whiny ogre mouth." Anya sat down in front of him. "Put your hands behind my waist and hang on."

"If you insist, but don't get any ideas. I'm only doing this for my own safety. I won't enjoy it one bit. So what is so special about his drag—*ulp*!"

Cinder lifted off, and Grey Cloak's stomach dropped into his toes. In a matter of seconds, they were hundreds of feet in the air. He hung onto Anya for dear life.

"What are you trying to do? Break me in half?"

"No, I'm trying not to chuck my biscuits!"

"Don't you dare!"

"Don't worry, I don't think I have anything left." He leaned over and peered at the diminishing land. *Me, a Sky Rider. Insanity.*

The thought of Grey Cloak being a Sky Rider wasn't far-fetched, however. When he was a boy, back in Dark Mountain, being a Sky Rider or a Risker was what he was being groomed for. He and Dyphestive both were, but they were too young to begin the training called the ripening. Instead, they were slowly being groomed by doing demanding chores for the Riskers and their dragons. Grey Cloak had decided at an early age he wanted no part of it. To him, the Riskers were a bunch of bloated thunderheads.

It took months, even years, of coaxing, but he managed to convince Dyphestive that they needed to run. He chose Dyphestive for a reason. The burly boy was loyal, and they'd been together as long as he could remember. If there was one person that he could trust, it was him. *Getting Zora back is one thing, but getting Dyphestive will be another. I swear I'll come and get you, brother.*

For the time being, at least, he'd found a way to get Anya headed in the right direction. He found some gratification in that.

They were so far up that he couldn't even see the leaves on the trees. And his vision was keen. "Aren't we awfully high up? How do you expect us to see anybody?"

Anya turned her head to look over her shoulder. "We need to be high up. That makes it a lot more difficult for Cinder to be spotted. He's very large, you know."

"I know," he said. Despite the chilling heights, Cinder's body kept the saddle very warm. That warmth carried through the rest of Grey Cloak's body. "But how can we see who we are looking for?"

Cinder turned his great head around and said, "I'll see them. Tell me what I'm looking for."

"Simple. A horse-drawn wagon and a group of six people. And they couldn't be very far ahead from where you met me. A few leagues, maybe."

"Thank you." Cinder turned his head back toward the front. He flew on, making a wide pattern of circles.

"Is he really going to be able to find them in the night?" Grey Cloak asked as he stared downward. "It doesn't seem possible. At least not until the crack of dawn."

"Don't worry. Cinder will find them. It is his unique gift. He could spot a tick on a dog from a league—"

"Found them and some others too," Cinder said. "Now what, Anya?"

8

"Rise and shine!"

Zora's eyelids snapped open, and the half-elf looked straight into the eyes of Hawk, the tall man she'd knocked out with her Ring of Mist. He was leering at her. She was lying in a wagon with her wrists bound behind her back and her ankles roped up too.

"Did you sleep well, Princess?" the rough-looking man asked. "Huh-huh."

She scooted up into a sitting position. It was morning twilight, her limbs were stiff, and she was cold from all of the rain. She'd had to sit in it all night, without any cover, and though she'd managed to catnap on and off, she felt horrible.

The scruffy little woman named Squirrel sauntered over to the wagon. She had an eerie look in her eyes and tapped her ring finger on the wagon's side. "Thanks for the ring, dearie. It's a true find." She smiled, showing a mouthful of crooked teeth.

Zora snarled. The Ring of Mist was her most precious find. She'd retrieved it on her first adventures with Talon, and Dalsay had let her keep it. The ring's small face was shaped like a pink daisy. It contained a magical knockout mist. "I'm surprised you could cram it on that stubby finger of yours."

"Stubby?" Squirrel's voice cracked like an old woman's.

Hawk huffed out a dry chuckle. "Ha! Even though she got the drop on me, I like her." He locked his big paw of a hand underneath Zora's chin. "And she's very pretty. We could use some nicer flowers in this group. The ladies in our midst are getting long in the tooth."

Katrina walked by and swatted Hawk in the behind with her sword.

Hawk's face lit up, and he nearly jumped out of his boots. "Yeow!" He pulled a dagger out and turned on Katrina.

Katrina dusted her long strands of brown and dyed-green hair from her eyes and gave him a daring look. "Stop making a fool of yourself, Hawk. That little ferret fooled you once. I bet she'll fool you again."

"Will not. And you need to mind your business and keep your sword to yourself," Hawk said.

"Are you challenging me again?" Katrina asked. "Why,

we haven't even made it past breakfast, and you want to take a crack at me." She eyed his dagger. "Once again, your shortcomings are obvious." She glanced at Zora. "Take note of that."

Hawk lifted his chin and snorted then snaked his dagger back into his sword belt. "Enjoy your position while it lasts. It won't be long." He marched away.

Katrina made her way over to the wagon. She leaned her back against it with her elbows propped up in front of Zora. "He likes you. Zora, is it?"

Zora didn't say a word. The demise of her friends had begun to sink in. They'd all been burned alive. The Scourge had murdered them.

"Oh, the poor dear is probably at a loss of words," Squirrel said. She was in her thirties, but she talked like an old lady. "After all, we did just cook her family."

Zora lunged at Squirrel. "You shut your mouth, you filthy rodent!"

Squirrel laughed in Zora's face. "What are you going to do? Bite me?"

"What's going on over here?" the short-haired Sash asked in a rugged voice. He was the strapping fish-eyed leader of the Scourge. He wore black sashes on his arms and one around his waist.

"Nothing, Captain," Squirrel said with a snicker. "Only having some fun."

"Fun's over. Load up your horses. It's time to head

north." He gave Katrina a stern look. "That means the both of you."

"Aye, aye, Captain," Katrina said as she drifted away.

Once the coast was clear, Sash turned his attention to Zora. "Listen here, little bird. Count your blessings that you live. And you live because of me. I could have roasted you like the others, but I didn't." He made a sucking sound through his teeth. "The Scourge could use a girl like you."

"Stuff it."

"Use that fire. You'll need it." He drummed his calloused hands on the side of the wagon. "Is it really true that Adanadel and Dalsay are dead?"

She didn't see the harm in telling him that they were, but she didn't want to make it easy on him, so she buttoned up.

"Answer me, girl."

She glared at him and said, "Yeah, they're dead. Now all of them are, aside from me. Does that make you happy, murderer?"

"The truth is, I didn't get as much satisfaction as you would think. I would have rather killed Adanadel myself. Huh. He kicked me out of Talon, you know. Said I was evil. Imagine that. Me, evil." He adjusted the sash that was tied around his bicep. "I'm a businessman, that's all. And I'm paid to do a job at any cost. If someone gets in my way, I eliminate them. Does that sound unreasonable?"

"You don't look like a reasonable person."

"I suppose I don't." He made that sucking sound through his teeth again as he looked about. "You know, just because I hated Talon doesn't mean that I didn't respect them. I didn't have a bone to pick with all of you. You weren't around back then. Think about it this way, little bird. I'm giving you a second chance out of respect for them. You would be wise to make the most of it, or else you'll wind up dead like them."

"Or *you* will."

"Death hasn't made me any promises that I know of." He moseyed away from the wagon. "Everybody, saddle up! We've got a long road ahead but a huge payday at the end. Long live the Scourge!"

All of the members hollered back, "Long live the Scourge!"

Zora's nimble fingers started working at her bonds. *I have to get out of here. They're crazy!*

9

ora's sharp nails picked at the cords holding her fast. Her fingernails had been hardened and coated with crushed gemstone dust. It was a process that Tanlin had taught her. Regardless, she was still a long way from cutting free, but she didn't need to rush at the moment.

The wagon moved along steadily over the bumpy road, making its way down toward the plains. It rocked from side to side because of the dips and ruts as it navigated the dark ridges through the tree line. A huge man named Bull was driving the wagon. He was all muscle and no neck, and he didn't say a word or turn around.

Squirrel was riding behind the wagon, accompanied by the wizard, Honzur. He was a mysterious-looking man dressed in ornate robes, and he had a nasty scar on his face. His hands were covered in tattoos, his fingers covered with many rings. The frail man's eyes were shut, but his lips moved as he mouthed words.

The sight of Honzur made Zora's skin crawl. She looked away and leaned over the front of the wagon. Hawk had taken point and was riding several dozen yards in front of the wagon. Sash and Katrina were riding side by side, only a few yards in front. The only other living creature in the group, aside from Zora, was the dragon, which was inside a covered cage. It never made a sound.

Zora curled up and lay down in the wagon. She was damp, and it was cold. Worst of all, she hadn't even had time to mourn the loss of her friends. Tanlin was dead, and he'd been like a father to her. And Grey Cloak, whom she'd become very fond of, was dead too. She sniffled and shivered. It wasn't fair. They hadn't even been trying to hurt anybody, but they were dead, and she was a prisoner.

The wagon came to a slow stop near the bottom of the black hills. Bull grunted like a hungry bear. Zora twisted up and looked over the side. With the bright morning sun in her eyes, she squinted.

"What is it, Hawk?" Sash hollered.

"People," Hawk replied.

"Well, it's a road. There's going to be people," Sash said. "What's so special about them?"

"These people are supposed to be dead."

"Say again?" Sash started moving his horse forward.

Zora scooted toward the front of the wagon and rose to

her knees. She had a full view of the road ahead. Standing fifty yards away were the dwarf, Rhonna, and the half-orc, Lythlenion. A tall woman with flowing auburn hair wearing a brilliant suit of plate-mail armor was standing between them. Zora's heart fluttered. *They're alive. But where are Grey Cloak and Tanlin?*

"Well, well, well," Sash said in his loud, boisterous voice. "I'm impressed that I didn't kill all of you. It looks like you have a new one too. What is the name of this vision?"

"Anya," the strong-voiced woman replied. "If you want to live, you will turn over your prisoner and your wagon."

"Is that so? Well, pretty lady, I think that you might want to realize that you are still outnumbered by a great deal."

Honzur trotted his horse to Sash and whispered to the bigger man.

Sash's big eyes widened. "Oh, I see. You are Anya the Sky Rider, is that so?"

"I am," she said.

Sash checked the skies. "Interesting, I don't see a dragon."

"Nor will you, because I don't have one with me," Anya said. "It seems that you have kidnapped a colleague of mine. We are here to take her back."

Bull turned and glowered down at Zora. He pulled a dagger from his belt and poked it toward her face. Zora crept back and managed to lean over the side. Her nails dug deeper into her bonds.

"Interesting company you keep," Sash said.

"I could say the same about you. Are you accustomed to traveling with a bunch of fools?"

"Heh. Aren't you a funny one?" Sash leaned over his saddle horn and said, "How much will you give me for the little woman?"

"I'm offering you your life," Anya said. She pulled her longsword. "All of your lives for hers."

Sash nodded. "So that's how you want to play it, huh. You know, I've always wanted to cross swords with a Sky Rider. You see, I've figured they are nothing but talk, unless they have their precious dragon." He looked up for a moment. "I can't help but feel that more eyes than yours are on me."

"If you want to fight me over the girl, then by all means, let's fight."

Bull rose and said, "Let me fight her! I'll crush the little woman!" He lifted a strange weapon that looked like a heavy club and had a long blade running down one side and a curved blade-hook at the tip of the other.

"Sit down," Sash said. "You know, Anya, a woman like you is out of her element. We are in Ugrad now."

"Thank you for the geography lesson." She advanced. "Now, let my friend go."

Sash spit over the side of his saddle and rubbed the

stubble on his chin. "No, I don't think I'm going to do that. As a matter of fact, I think I'll offer you an even better deal. I'll exchange Zora for you. How does that sound?"

"It sounds a like a fantasy that your big ego will never fulfill."

"We'll see about that. Scourge, take her!"

10

Not only did Cinder spot the Scourge, but he sniffed out what was left of Talon as well. The dragon landed, the reunion was brief, and the group soon worked up a plan that included a stone-faced elven ranger named Bowbreaker, whom Grey Cloak had never met before.

The goal was simple: free Zora and the crypt dragon with as little commotion as possible. That would mean that Cinder wouldn't play a part on the ground, but he would watch from high in the sky. It was dangerous enough that they were in Dark Mountain territory. If they were discovered, it would be fatal.

Grey Cloak was hidden in the ledges of the rocky woodland. Tanlin and Bowbreaker were with him, keeping an eye on things from a close distance. From his spot, he could hear Anya and Sash's unpleasant conversation.

"That's one tough lady," Tanlin said. "I'm glad she's on our side." His slender hands toyed with the scarf around his neck. "I'm ready to go in."

"Hold on. That woman, Squirrel, is still lingering toward the rear. Wait for her to move away."

Bowbreaker had an arrow nocked. His intense eyes were locked on Sash. "If I kill him, the rest will scatter. I can do it now."

"Let's see what Anya can get out of them," Grey Cloak said.

Sash ordered his company, "Scourge, take her!"

Bowbreaker raised his bow, pulling the string back to run the arrow's feathers along his cheek. The rippling sinew in his arms held the bow rock steady.

"Hold," Grey Cloak said.

At that same moment, Squirrel moved toward the front of the wagon, and Bull got out of the seat.

"Go, Tanlin."

Tanlin pulled his scarf up over his nose. His face and the rest of his body and garments disappeared. He made faint footprints in the ground and was off and running.

"I still have a good shot," Bowbreaker said.

"Not until Zora is clear. I'm not worried about the dragon, but she has to be safe."

"You are fond of her."

"She's my friend."

"The tension in your voice reveals that she's more than a friend to you. How does she feel?"

Grey Cloak gave him a surprised look. "Who are you?"

"Bowbreaker."

"You're very strange, Bowbreaker."

The Scourge circled Anya, Lythlenion, and Rhonna.

Grey Cloak started to grind his teeth. He wasn't sure how well Anya could handle so many enemies at once, but she'd made it perfectly clear that she was fully confident she could handle them. He checked the sky. No sign of Cinder. *You'd better be right, Anya.*

ANYA'S SWORD started to shimmer like lightning. The blinding light glared in the Scourge's eyes. All of them shielded their eyes behind their arms.

"Are you certain that you want to try to take me? I don't think that would be wise. After all, you cannot hit what you cannot see."

"And I thought this was going to be a sword fight. It's no surprise that you resorted to tricks." Sash fought to keep his horse from stomping new mudholes into the ground. "Krackens, Honzur! Do something!"

Honzur was sitting on his perfectly calm horse with his arms hanging at his sides. A dreary mist began to ebb from his fingers. Its soft inky darkness filled the area and dulled the shining power of the sword.

Sash regained control of his horse, and with an ugly grin, he said, "Perfect." He pointed his sword at Anya. "Take them!" He spurred his horse forward. "Eeeyah!"

"SHOOT HIM!" Grey Cloak said to Bowbreaker.

"I would if not for the bright spots in my eyes. I didn't anticipate that," the elven ranger replied.

Grey Cloak couldn't disagree. The blinding light had caused dark spots in his eyes. He blinked repeatedly and shook his head. By the time the spots had cleared from his eyes, the Scourge was locked in mortal combat with his comrades. His feet took on a life of their own, and he sprinted toward the fray.

ZORA'S FINGERNAILS sawed deeper into her cords. She wiggled the loosening bonds, creating deeper rope burns on her wrists. A bright flash of light nearly blinded her, but she had her back to it. *Come on. Get out of these ropes!*

"Do you need a hand, little flower?" someone said in a soft voice.

She looked about. "Tanlin?"

"Either that or the ghost of Tanlin. Turn around and be still." He cut her cords free.

Even though she couldn't see him, she could feel him, and she hugged him like a child hugging a parent in the black of night. With the commotion of battle growing nearby, she squeezed him tight and said, "You're alive. Thank goodness you're alive!"

"We all are," he said.

"Even Grey Cloak?"

"Yes."

She squeezed him tight again.

"Not so hard—you'll reveal me." Tanlin lifted the canvas covering the dragon's cage.

Zora pushed his hand down. "What are you doing? Trying to get us hypnotized?"

"You need to run. East of here. To the woodland. Grey Cloak is there. As for the dragon, I need to free it. Don't worry. I'll avert my eyes." His invisible hands lifted the canvas, revealing a metal padlock on the cage door. "Now get to safety! Go!"

"I'm not leaving you. Besides, I'm a much better lock picker than you are." She fished a pick out of the thick strands of her hair. "See? Let me try." She could feel his hands, even though she couldn't see them. "Will you move? I'll be done in a moment."

"Well, well, well, look who slipped her knots."

Zora turned and faced Squirrel. The mousy woman was standing behind the wagon with a hand crossbow pointed dead at her.

Squirrel gave a winning smile. "Raise those hands and don't move."

11

Anya deftly sidestepped Sash's charge and sliced across the straps of his saddle. The saddle broke free, and Sash tumbled to the ground. The rush of horse hooves caught her attention, and she ducked as a sword slice whistled over her head. A tall warrior charged by then turned his horse.

"Eeeyarg!" A third attacker, a woman with dyed-green hair, raced toward Anya on the back of her steed.

Anya jumped clear over the charging horse and the woman then flipped upside down and winked at the woman, who mouthed, "Whoa." She landed on her feet just in time to catch Sash rushing at her.

Sash fought two-handed with his longsword made from blackened steel. He swung with force, and his and Anya's sword blades banged together loudly. The light in Anya's sword went dim. They danced back and forth, blades weaving, stabbing, and banging.

"You fight like a lion!" Sash commented as he thrust, missed, and thrust again. "I admire it greatly!"

"You should." Anya moved over the bumpy ground gracefully. She gripped her sword with only one hand, and she fought like a champion fencer. "I am your superior!" With a twist of her wrist, she ripped Sash's sword out of his hands, and it stuck in the ground nearby.

Sash swallowed and dropped to his knees then lifted his hands and wiggled his fingers. "You are the master. I surrender."

Hawk charged from one side and Katrina from the other, and Anya jumped straight up in the air. Both horses and riders collided, and the horses tumbled over.

"You idiots!" Sash ran for his sword and snatched it out of the ground then faced Anya. "Shall we dance again, grasshopper?"

"You aren't much of a dancer."

"Let's see how I do this time." He rolled a finger, and the sashes around his arms and waist slithered away from his body like snakes. The silky black garments slid over the ground, straight toward Anya's feet, moving very fast.

Anya cut through the first ribbon, but the other ribbons leapt from the ground and snared her arms. In a split second, they were coiling and restricting all over her body. They fastened to roots and pulled her to the ground.

One sash coiled around her neck, and she started choking.

Sash laughed. "I bet you're not feeling so high and mighty now, are you, Sky Rider?" Sword in hand, he closed the gap between them. "Say good night forever!"

RHONNA JUMPED AWAY from Bull's edged club. The nasty weapon bit into the ground and sparked on the rocks. She rolled to one knee, raised her hammer, and awaited the brute's charge.

Lythlenion stepped into the lumbering giant's path and hit Bull in the chest with an old mace he'd purchased in Daggerford. But the muscle-bound man didn't so much as grunt.

"Oh dear," Lythlenion said.

Bull pinned Lythlenion's arm and head-butted the cleric in the face. "Hah! You think orc heads are hard. Bull's head is harder."

"You can say that again," Lythlenion said as he stumbled backward. He took a knee and shook his head. "Oof, that hurt. I haven't been head-butted like that in a decade."

Bull lifted his war club over his head and prepared to smash it down fully on Lythlenion's skull.

"No, you don't!" Rhonna whipped her hammer through the air. It sailed true and hit Bull square in the beans.

Bull's lazy eyes grew wide, and he let out an angry scream.

"Right in the nanoos! Well done, Rhonna!" Lythlenion said. He gathered his feet under him and charged Bull.

Together, Rhonna and Lythlenion bore the bigger man down to the ground. The trio wrestled over the wet ground like crocodiles in a mud pit. Bull could fight, and true to his name, he was as strong as a bull too.

A fierce punch from Bull made Rhonna's teeth clack. A vicious elbow put a dent in Lythlenion's breastplate. The battle lasted agonizing seconds before Bull had them both pinned in the mud by the neck.

Rhonna's face started to sink into a muddy puddle. She whaled on Bull's big arm with her hammer, but without a good angle to strike at the arm, she couldn't muster enough fire behind the blow. A victorious sneer built on Bull's face. The ugly man stoked the furnace within her, and her mud-coated fingers reached for a dagger tied against her leg. She yanked it out and stabbed Bull in the thigh.

Bull let out a loud "Yeeeoup!" and jumped away.

Rhonna and Lythlenion gasped and spit muddy water. They came to their feet with their chests heaving, and they looked at one another then eyed Bull, who was crawling through the mud toward his weapon.

"Can you still do it?" she asked Lythlenion.

"Of course I can, but I need time," he replied.

"I'll give you all the time I can." She marched toward

Bull with her hammer in hand. "Oy! Big fella, what's the problem? Can't you smash a little dwarf like me?" As she talked, she could hear Lythlenion muttering. "Come on then. Finish me!"

Bull picked up his weapon with a snarl on his face. The hulking brute looked like a mud-covered abomination, muscles heaving. Even with a hole in his leg, he didn't limp when he moved. It was a testament to his savage nature. "Bull will kill you, rodent."

Rhonna had no doubt that he could. He was twice as tall as she was and was three times her width. It was the type of moment in which she would have relied on Griff, her half-orc and half-ogre friend who Drysis had killed for no reason. Griff had lived for such a fight. She rolled her hammer in the air. "Well, bring it on then!"

Bull charged, and Rhonna braced for impact.

12

Zora lifted her hands and faced Squirrel. "Well, look who broke away from the fight. The ugly little Squirrel. What are you going to do? Tie me up again?"

Squirrel gave a crooked smile. "No, I think I'm going to shoot you this time. It's nothing personal." She had the hand crossbow aimed right at Zora's chest. "I just don't like you."

The canvas that covered the dragon cage slowly dropped back into place, as if it had a life of its own.

"Say, how'd you do that?" Squirrel asked. Suddenly, her hand crossbow began smacking her in the head repeatedly. Her knees wobbled. Something invisible knocked her in the jaw, and down she went. She lay on the ground, out cold.

The hand crossbow rose from the ground, and Tanlin

reappeared. He shook his hand and grimaced. "She might not look like much, but she has a very firm jaw." He pulled his scarf down. "Now, get that lock picked while I tie her up."

Zora nodded. Without word, she lifted the canvas draped over the cage and closed her eyes. *I'm not going to look at that dragon again. The last time left me with an awful headache.* She grabbed the lock. The keyhole was at the bottom. She stuck her hairpin, which was custom-made into a lockpick, into the mechanism.

"Hurry up. The battle isn't going so well," Tanlin whispered harshly.

"I am," she said. Zora didn't need to see the lock to open it. It was all about feeling. Her fingers and the lockpick became one. She could feel every little tumbler inside the lock, and slowly, she began picking and twisting away at them. *This is a hard one.* The sounds of battle caused her forehead to bead with sweat. Her heart pounded in her ears. *Zooks, what is this lock made of?*

"Zora, we are running out of time," Tanlin said urgently.

"Hold your horses!" The padlock popped. "Got it!" She yanked the padlock off and chucked it away. "Look away. I'm going to open the door." She pulled open the cage door and awkwardly hid behind it, but she didn't hear so much as a sound. No scrape or scuffle of dragon claws, and she'd heard those memorable sounds before. She peeked out of one eye.

The ivory-colored dragon was lying curled up in its cage like a sleeping dog. Its head was tucked inside its wing. Zora banged on the cage, but the dragon didn't budge. She shook the cage, but that still had no effect.

"Tanlin, the dragon is sleeping. What do I do?" She turned her head. "Tanlin?"

He was suspended in midair. His chin was dropped onto his chest, his body hanging limp. The wizard, Honzur, was standing beside him, his hands glowing with green fire.

The hairs on Zora's arms rose. "Tanlin!"

"You are very clever, girl," Honzur said in his mysterious voice. "But not clever enough. You see, that dragon is under my control." He lifted his right hand, which was holding a large gemstone that was burning green. It was a dragon charm. "Now, if you will, close that cage door and put the lock back on."

The lock, which she'd tossed into the grass, floated over before her eyes and dropped into her hands. She swallowed the lump in her dry throat and asked, "And if I don't?"

"I'll kill your friend," the vulture-like Honzur replied.

Zora slowly started to close the door.

"That's a good girl. You are very wise. Very pretty—*Ack!*"

An arrow ripped into Honzur's back and stuck between

his shoulder blades. He fell onto his knees, grimacing and gasping. The dragon charm fell from his fingers. Tanlin fell to the ground.

The dragon's head popped up, then it rose and slunk out of the cage. Zora shielded herself behind the door and watched the dragon spread its wings and launch into the air. It took off toward the clouds like it had been shot out of a crossbow.

Zora slid out of the wagon. Honzur's fingers were outstretched as he reached for the dragon charm. She stepped on his hand and picked up the charm. "Looking for this?" She eyed the arrow in Honzur's back. It had black feathers. She traced its flight path back to a very large elf carrying a longbow and walking out of the woodland. Her heart thumped. *Lords of the Air. Who is that?*

13

Rhonna didn't stand a chance against the brutish Bull, and she knew it. He might be dumb, but he was a natural fighter. When he swung, he swung to kill. But he had a weakness—he telegraphed his swings. She knew where they were going before they were coming. Bull chopped from the left, and she jumped to the right. He chased her right, and she dodged left.

The dance went on, and Bull put more force into every swing. "Stand still, you fat grasshopper!" He swung his club down, and it hit the ground where she had been standing and sank into the mud. When he pulled it out, it made a sucking sound.

Rhonna paused to catch her breath. She was nimble for a dwarf and a clever fighter, but Bull's blows were getting closer. She hollered at Lythlenion as Bull closed the gap between them with his club held high. "Lyth! Are you ready?"

"I have you now!" Bull roared.

Rhonna prepared to jump, but her boots were sunk deep in the mud. She was stuck. Bull's club came down.

Bong! A huge fist made of mystic energy collided with Bull's body and knocked him through the air.

Lythlenion stood in front of Rhonna with his fists at his sides, glowing with citrine-colored mystic energy. They were the size of pumpkins. "I'll take it from here." He marched over to Bull, who was rising from the muddy ground, and started hammering away on the brute with resounding blows. *Boom! Boom! Boom! Boom!*

Bull sank into the mud. He didn't rise again.

ANYA TWISTED and squirmed against Sash's ribbons, which were coiling around her neck and holding her wrists fast. She had to hand it to Sash—the greasy fighter was clever. He'd bought just enough time to slay her. *This can't be it! I'm not supposed to die like this. I haven't avenged my parents!*

Sash cocked his sword arm back and delivered the lethal stroke.

GREY CLOAK DASHED over the wet ground at full speed toward the battle, watching in horror as his friends were locked in mortal combat. He couldn't help all of them at once. As he took in the grueling scene, he focused on Anya.

The Sky Rider was tethered by black sashes. Her face was beet red, and she was choking to death. The man attacking her was Sash, and he had murder in his eyes as he closed in.

No! I can't let this happen. I won't let this happen! Grey Cloak's long legs were in full stride. But he was only elven, so he couldn't cross the distance in time. He had to move quicker. *Faster, legs! Faster!*

All of a sudden, Grey Cloak's legs took on a life of their own. They propelled him forward at an inhuman speed. Faster than a speeding horse, he galloped and kept gaining speed. An exhilarating feeling flowed through him like lightning coursing through his veins. *What is happening?* A split second from Sash running his sword through Anya, he blindsided the man at full speed. *Crunch!*

Sash's body went skidding over the ground, his sword flying from his fingers. He lay on the ground, knocked out cold.

"How did you do that?" Anya asked as she pulled the limp ribbons away from her neck. She loosened the ones on her arms as well.

"I don't know," he said as he looked blankly at his feet.

The energy that had flowed through him was gone, and he felt drained.

"You ran like the wind. It was impressive." Anya bent down and kissed his cheek. "I'm in your debt."

He rubbed his cheek. "You're welcome."

RHONNA, Tanlin, and Zora hog-tied every last member of the Scourge and secured them all to the wagon. Lythlenion retrieved his war mace.

Zora wrested her ring from Squirrel and said, "I'll be taking this back, Varmint Face."

The only member of the Scourge needing serious medical attention was Honzur. The arrow was still in his back. Lythlenion removed it and applied treatment.

Bowbreaker was standing nearby, watching, and said, "I am perplexed. He shouldn't be breathing, but he is."

Lythlenion stuffed a gag into Honzur's mouth and made sure that the wizard's hands were bound tightly. "Don't be surprised. I've seen mages with skin thicker than metal. I'm certain he has some sort of protection draped over him. It will take more than an ordinary arrow to kill the likes of him."

"We should kill all of them, after what they did to us," Rhonna suggested. She glared at Sash. "If we ever meet again, I will."

"Huh-huh-huh. Next time, if I see you first, you'll all be dead."

"We should have killed them in battle," Anya added. "But that wasn't the plan." She searched the sky. "Freeing the dragon was, and he's gone. Your friend is saved too. We must go."

The company called Talon gathered all of the gear and the horses, leaving the Scourge with nothing but their ropes and wagon. They headed south hastily and didn't look back.

Inside the shadowy channels of the Dark Ridges, Zora cozied up to Grey Cloak and walked her horse with him, shoulder to shoulder. "So much has happened that I forgot to thank you."

"Oh, well, it wasn't all me," he said with a smile. "Only mostly me."

She gave a pleasant laugh and said, "Who is that elf carrying a bow?"

He raised his eyebrows. "That's Bowbreaker. A friend of Rhonna and Lythlenion, I believe. He's very odd."

"Odd? Why do you say that? I think he's very handsome."

"Handsome? How can you say that? If he smiled, his face would crack. Like Rhonna's."

"I don't know. There is something mysterious about him."

Grey Cloak's eye twitched. *Does she like that boorish elf*

more than me? Impossible. "Well, if you like elves that sleep in the woodland and keep company with wild critters, I think you'll be well matched with him. He enjoys eating bugs too."

She made a horrified expression. "Bugs?"

"Well, yes. You know, he sort of lives off the land. He doesn't care for the pleasantries of civilization." He laid it on thick. "Look at his clothing. Buckskin. He probably killed a baby deer to make it. That sort of skin is softer. And he probably doesn't wash regularly or scrub his teeth. You know, very barbaric."

Her face continued to sour. "I can't say, but I've not been close enough to him to notice."

"I would keep my distance. Or at least take time to get used to it. He's the kind of man that blends in with nature, and when nature calls, well, you know."

"That's disgusting. Are you telling me that he covers himself in filth?"

"Only when necessary. Of course, I'm assuming that, but well, once you're downwind of him, you'll get the idea."

"That's a shame because he's very handsome."

"If you think so." Grey Cloak ground his teeth.

Anya wandered back from the front and stopped Grey Cloak from advancing. "It's time for us to go."

He shook his head. "I'm not going anywhere. Not until I get Dyphestive."

14

Grey Cloak and Anya were standing in the middle of the muddy pass, having a full-blown argument. Blue veins stood out on her temples, and her cheeks were bloodred. They were surrounded by the company.

"You said that you would come after this rescue. You gave your word!" Anya said.

"I never said that. You only helped so you could save your dragon. You couldn't have cared less about Zora!" he fired back. "Where is your little dragon, anyway?" He looked up. "Hah! It flew away."

"Listen to me." Anya's voice was icy. "You don't have a choice. You have to come. And all I have to do is call Cinder down here to snatch you up. Now quit acting like a spoiled child and come along quietly."

"We are going after Dyphestive!" He crossed his arms over his chest and turned his back. "Period."

Anya shook her head. Her beautiful face was distraught. "Can't any of you talk some sense into him? He is not ready to go to Dark Mountain, and neither are the likes of you. Black Frost and his dragons will char you to the bone once he sniffs you out. You know this."

The Sky Rider was met with averted eyes.

She turned to Tanlin. "You are a Servant of the Wind. Can you help me get through to them?"

Tanlin's arms were crossed, and his chin was tucked in his hand. "Perhaps a more thorough explanation will suffice. After all, I think we deserve it. And to be truthful, I'm disappointed that it took a dragon to coax you in our favor over my comrade Zora. What was so special about that crypt dragon?"

"He is not a crypt dragon. Crypt dragons have dark eyes. This dragon is more than that. He's an ivory dragon with the rare ability to control other dragons. Black Frost could use that dragon to control any dragon, at least with the help of the dragon charm." Anya removed her helmet and brushed her damp hair away from her eyes. "Ivory dragons are very independent and private."

"So this dragon could be used against Black Frost's armies," Tanlin asked.

"It could. But I imagine it will move on and burrow far, far away."

"Why don't we use the dragon charm on it?"

"It's too late now. It's gone. That's all that matters. The charms are good for keeping dragons from attacking, or even befriending them, but we try not to use them unless needed. We don't abuse them like Black Frost. The important thing is that we removed a very powerful weapon from Black Frost's arsenal."

"I see," Tanlin said.

Anya pointed at Grey Cloak. "He is a natural, the son of Zanna Paydark, a Sky Rider like me. He needs to return with me, to the Sky Riders, and prepare for his destiny."

Grey Cloak rolled his eyes. "I don't have a destiny. But I do have a date to save Dyphestive." He scanned the group. "Who is with me?"

Rhonna stepped forward. "Listen, Grey Cloak, I'm willing to find Dyphestive, no matter the risk, but she's right. We aren't ready. *You* aren't ready. I think it would be best if you went with her while we search out Dyphestive."

"Are you serious? You are siding with her. This woman with delusions of grandeur. All she wants to do is kill Black Frost. Did she tell you that? Huh? She's obsessed with killing him because he killed her parents."

"He killed your parents too!" Anya said.

"I don't even know my parents. How do I even know that Zanna Paydark is my mother? Is that because *you* say so? Can you even prove it?"

Anya's jaw dropped. "Do you really think that I would

go to all of this trouble over you if that weren't so? Of course she was your mother. The Lords of the Air said so." She rubbed her head. "Talking to you makes my mind ache."

Rhonna stuck a cigar in her mouth and said, "If you say you are a man, then stop acting like a child. You need to learn the truth about yourself. It's not every day that a boy like you gets to learn where he comes from."

"It's not that. I have to save Dyphestive. I promised. We can't leave him out there with them." He gestured north. "I can't do that. He needs me."

"Listen," Rhonna said. "This isn't my first campaign. Lyth and I know a lot about Ugrad. Let us figure out what happened to Dyphestive. The first thing we need to know is that he's alive. Proof of life, even though I hate to say that. You need to trust us. In the meantime, go with Anya. Prepare to be a dragon rider or whatever."

Grey Cloak twisted toward Anya and said, "How long does this training take?"

She lifted her shoulders and said, "I don't know. You have passed the stage of ripening. My guess would be that it would take at least a year or two."

"*A year or two?*"

Rhonna fastened her stubby fingers on his elbow and squeezed hard. "Listen to me. Sometimes in life you have to do what you have to do. You don't always get a choice. Now, you might think that this is all about you, but the truth is, it's about all of us. Black Frost and his armies are wicked. You know this. You've seen it for yourself. You ran from it. Well, you can't always run. Sometimes you have to stand. Stand with us. Stand for Dyphestive. We'll do our part and meet you in Loose Boot in one year. And if you aren't there, we'll meet the next year. But we will be there. At least *I* will be. I swear it."

"You would do anything to get rid of me, wouldn't you?" he joked.

Rhonna replied, "You know it."

15

The flight on Cinder was long, and Grey Cloak's back ached. Even though the dragon's flight was smooth and easy compared to the last one, Grey Cloak stayed clammed up the entire time, as he wasn't in any mood for talking. He'd already done most of the talking by yelling, and his throat was sore.

I can't believe I let Rhonna talk me into this. What sort of fool am I? He'd always considered himself a persuasive sort, but this time Rhonna persuaded him. He didn't like being forced to do something that he didn't want to do. The mere thought of it gnawed at his stomach.

Grey Cloak was living a life that bards wrote great songs about, riding on the back of a flying dragon with a beautiful woman. But he couldn't have cared less. Instead, his mind kept wandering. *What is Zora doing?*

Just when he was getting close to the nubile thief, Anya had found a way to yank her out of his arms. Worst of all, Zora had shown interest in Bowbreaker. The elven ranger was a perfect specimen of an elf. A super specimen, perhaps. Much like Grey Cloak, he was well-built but taller and even more muscular. Bowbreaker was handsome, too, but he had the personality of a mudhole, whereas Grey Cloak abounded in charm.

What does she see in him? I have to wait a year, maybe two, to see her again? Why, they could be married! No! Impossible!

"Easy with those tongs," Anya said.

He didn't realize what she was talking about at first, then he noticed that his fingers were digging into her waist. He eased his grip and looked over the side. He was fine riding the dragon, but when he looked down, he became queasy, though not as badly as before.

"Are you still brooding?" Anya asked.

"No." *Yes. Of course I am.*

"I guess you miss that little part-elf, don't you?"

How did she know that? He looked at her dragon-fashioned helm. *Can she read minds like that?* "Of course not. Don't be silly."

"Oh, come now, I saw the way you looked at her and how you pleaded your case on her behalf. You like her very much, don't you?"

"Even if I did, it doesn't make much of a difference now, does it? I won't see her again for years."

"True love will wait." She glanced over her shoulder and smiled. "I can help."

"Help with what?"

"Women. I can give you advice."

"You, the dragon lady? I hardly think you are the one to be giving me advice on dating."

"Ah, you do sound interested."

"No, I'm only making a general statement. And what would you know about courting anyone? All you talk about is vengeance. I'm sure you would be a pure delight at the dining table."

"You have a very sharp tongue," she said.

"It goes with my wit."

"Well, if you aren't interesting in learning how to woo Zora, then I'll leave you alone. But know this—you are going about it the wrong way."

"If you say so."

After a pause, Anya said, "You see, there is your problem. You don't always have to get the last word in. You don't have to show off your wit. Be yourself."

He threw his hands out and said, "I *am* being myself."

"No, you are hiding behind a smart mouth. There is a difference. Lower your guard. And pardon my expression, but be more human. Women appreciate sincerity."

"If you say so."

Anya sighed. "See, you did it again."

"I know I did. I said it. And I said it because I want you

to stop talking about it." He thought about jumping off the dragon to get away. *Perhaps my cloak will break my fall. Like it did at Lovers' Gorge.*

Cinder's flight lowered through the fields of clouds. Endless leagues of green hills and rocky mountains and a great lake were below them. He flew even lower and started to glide. The hazy sun had begun to set.

"Are we landing?" Grey Cloak asked.

"Yes," Anya replied.

"Where are we exactly?"

"We'll be landing in the hills behind Salt Knob. We'll await my uncle Justus there."

"The sooner we land, the better. Do you think we can get some food?"

"Are you asking me out to dinner?"

"Ha-ha. You, never."

Cinder landed on a bald knob surrounded by great oak and maple trees at the top. They weren't alone, either. Waiting on the ground for them were another dragon rider and his dragon.

The dragon rider had his dragon helm tucked under his arm. His hair and beard were brown with streaks of gray. He was wearing the same sort of plate-mail armor that Anya did, and it was well crafted and had a dull shine to it. The dragon he was standing in front of was not as big as Cinder but still a monster in size. She was a female dragon with eyelashes and lighter scales on her belly. Much like

Cinder, she had tortoise-like splashes of color that brightened her ruddy scales. Her color was a vibrant orange, whereas Cinder's was a mix of gold and red.

Anya hurried out of the dragon saddle and jumped most of the way down. She rushed into the man's arms. "Uncle Justus!"

Justus hugged her tight and picked her up off of her feet. He spoke with the voice of a caring father. "I'm glad that you are well. I was beginning to worry."

"You needn't worry about me. You know I'm a big girl who can take care of herself."

Justus set her down and said, "Of course." He glanced up at Grey Cloak and approached. "And who is this?"

"Grey Cloak," she said. "The son of Zanna Paydark. At least I believe he is."

"Hello. Why don't you come down so I can have a look at you?" Justus asked.

Grey Cloak jumped out of the saddle and hit the ground softly on his feet. He stood face-to-face with Justus. The older warrior had Adanadel's strong angular features, and he carried himself with an air of self-control. Even though Grey Cloak felt reluctant to introduce himself, he said politely, "Hello," and extended his hand.

Justus shook his hand with a firm grip and said, "You have your mother's eyes. It warms my heart to see them again. Welcome, young man. Now come, the Lords of the Air are waiting."

16

Sweat dripped into Dyphestive's eyes, stinging them. He didn't bother to wipe it away. It would only come back. He pushed a wheelbarrow full of coal lumps up a steady incline that twisted through Dark Mountain's lower hills. The northern air was chilly, but a fog-like steam was rolling down from the surrounding volcanoes and making a sweltering effect.

The wheelbarrow's wheel slid over into a rut. The cart tipped over, and half of the coal spilled out.

"You idiot!" Scar said in a biting voice. "Pick that load up. You're wasting time." He snapped the lash in his hand, making a loud *wupash!*

Dyphestive towed the cart over the rut and looked back at the man. Scar was wearing his black leather dragon-scale armor. His leather skeleton mask was off, revealing a face full of many red and puffy scars. His dark hair was combed back behind a straight hairline. For a man, he was ugly.

"What are you gawking at now? My pretty face?" Scar asked and cracked his lash again.

After licking his lips, Dyphestive said in a dry and raspy voice, "I was wondering when I could get some water."

"Water? Hah! You can drink when your chore is over. Now pick up that coal and get moving!" *Wupash!*

Carrying one in each hand, Dyphestive picked up the large lumps of coal and put them in the cart. His huge hands were black with soot, and so was his clothing. Since he'd arrived at Dark Mountain, he hadn't washed and had slept very little. The Doom Riders kept him busy with one meaningless backbreaking chore after the other. He filled the cart up and started pushing again.

"Stop taking your time and get up that hill!" Scar said.

Dyphestive ignored the comment. He ignored them all. Though he wasn't sure what Drysis the Dreadful and her brood were trying to do, he'd done his fair share of wearisome work before. He could take it.

As he passed through a network of bubbling pools, rivulets of lava flowed over the crater rims and cooled. A constant hissing sound was in the air. Sweat streamed down Dyphestive's body, and his drenched clothes clung to his chest.

"Will you hurry up? I hate the burning alley!" Scar ordered.

Dyphestive took his time. He could have pushed the cart much faster, but he wanted to make Scar suffer as much as him. Worse, if he could pull it off. *Heh-heh.*

He plodded over the grueling road, angling toward the top. The farther he went, the more his back ached and his legs burned. He kept pushing the heavy load, one foot after the other, determined not to break. That was what Drysis wanted, to break him.

But something else kept Dyphestive's legs churning—anger. The Doom Riders had killed his best friend and blood brother, Grey Cloak. He'd watched them kill his only other friends, too—Browning, Dalsay, and Adanadel. They were a murdering bunch of thugs, and he hated them. *I'm going to make them pay for it.* He told himself that over and again. It gave him strength and purpose that fueled his weary limbs.

Dyphestive pushed the wheelbarrow beyond the network of small volcanoes to a higher point, where the northern cold greeted him. Snowflakes were falling, and his sweat became ice, and his breath came out frosty. The trek through the mountains was a miserable situation, going from the heat to the cold, back and forth.

"Ah, I like that crisp air. It's refreshing," Scar said and tried to catch a snowflake on his tongue.

Though Dyphestive could have killed for a drink, he

dared not try to catch a frosty flake on his tongue. It didn't take much of an excuse for Scar to crack the nine-tailed lash over his back. He was the worst of the bunch, and Dyphestive was glad that the Doom Riders rotated between Scar, Shamrok, and Ghost. At least they had so far, but it had only been a few days.

He shoved the wheelbarrow up the steepest and final part of the climb. His arm and leg muscles bulged from the effort. The last heave sent the wheelbarrow over the top, and he paused to catch his breath.

"It's about time." Scar walked over the plateau and stretched out his arms then twisted his hips from side to side and unslung his canteen and started drinking. "Ah. Now that is good. Really, really good and still cold too."

Without giving the warrior so much as a glance, Dyphestive pushed the wheelbarrow to the edge of the plateau. It overlooked a deep gorge and sent a fiery river of lava down. He tilted the wheelbarrow up by the handles and dumped its contents over the rim. And he would do it all over again. It was a two-hour climb up the hill and a two-hour walk back down. He did it three times a day, leaving very little time for sleep.

"Are you ready for that drink?" Scar asked. He had two canteens slung over his shoulder and only drank from one.

Dyphestive nodded. At the same time, he noticed that Scar was standing dangerously close to the ledge. It wouldn't take much to push him into the chasm. He shuffled over to the man with his eyes down. *Do it, Dyphestive. Do it!*

17

Dyphestive reached for the canteen with his pulse pounding in his temples. He wanted Scar dead more than anybody. All he had to do was grab the canteen and shove the man forward at the same time. He took the canteen in his fingers, pulled it free, and walked away.

Scar gave a dry laugh. "You chickened out, didn't you? Hah. If I were you, I would want to kill me too." He had a dagger that had appeared out of nowhere in his hand, and he rolled it over his wrist and fingers. "It's a good thing that you didn't try. I would have killed you."

"Maybe, but I would throw us both over the rim first." He tipped the canteen to his lips and drank. It only had a swallow in it. He gave Scar a disappointed look and threw the canteen at the ground. "Give me the other."

Scar patted the other canteen on his hip and said, "This one is mine. That one was yours. You should have saved it."

"I hate you."

"Good. Now we have something in common." Scar looked out over the rim. Higher up in the mountains was Black Frost's castle. It was more or less a stark-looking monument, cut out of the mountain and shaped like a ziggurat. It appeared to overlook the entire world. "They'll never kill him."

Dyphestive picked up the canteen and tossed it into the wheelbarrow. He'd never heard Scar speak thoughtfully before and said, "I beg your pardon."

"Black Frost. They'll never kill him. They've all tried before and failed." Scar gave Dyphestive a knowing look. "The Wizards of the Watch have failed. The armies of Monarch City have failed. All who have tried have failed. Sky Riders. Giants. The Arrowwood elves. Hah, Black Frost laughs at them."

"Well, maybe they haven't tried everything. Everything has a weakness, right?"

"You saw him. He doesn't. He's more than scales and brawn. He's elemental. A part of nature itself. You can't stop the wind or the rain. It's the same with him. That's why I follow him."

"If he can't be stopped, then why did you come after us?"

Scar shrugged. "Black Frost is not a fool. He knows he

has enemies but always manages to stay a step ahead of them. It will be a glorious thing when he takes it all over. He'll set all of his true servants up like kings."

"That sounds wonderful." He started pushing the wheelbarrow back down the hill. "Can we go now?"

Scar turned his back on the ledge and marched back down the path without so much as a word. Dyphestive seized the opportunity to scoop a handful of snow from the rocks. He stuffed it in his mouth and wet his face with it. It gave him little relief, but as lonely and depressed as he was, he would take anything. He followed Scar back down the mountain, contemplating what the Doom Riders were up to. Black Frost had ordered Drysis to train him, but so far, she'd done nothing but torture him. He didn't understand what they were doing. *I won't let them break me.*

Drysis, Shamrok, and Ghost met them at the bottom of the mountain. Shamrok and Ghost were in their dragon-scale leather armor, though Shamrok's mask was off, showing his handsome, grinning face and short red hair. Ghost had left his dark-blue dyed-leather skull mask on. He *always* had it on. Drysis's white hair was swiped over the side of her head like a wave. She always had an eye patch over her left eye and wore the same black leather dragon-scale armor. The only difference was the metal chain mail covering her left arm and the pump-action crossbow hanging over her back.

Drysis had a cross look on her face. She always did.

"Brothers of Destruction, we need to meet. Shamrok, take Dyphestive to his quarters while Scar briefs me on today's events." She focused on Dyphestive. "You are finished for the day. Feed him and let him wash, perhaps."

"As you wish," Shamrok said. He grabbed Dyphestive by the nape of the neck. "Well, you heard her. Get moving."

Dyphestive didn't have to be told twice. He pushed the wheelbarrow toward the small barracks that he and the Doom Riders were staying in. But something was eating at his mind. The way that Drysis had spoken ate at him. Something had changed. He couldn't imagine that things would be worse, but it felt like it.

A shadow passed over him as scores of Riskers flew overhead in a V-formation. He saw them from time to time throughout the day, running drills through the sky. On more than one occasion, they had flown low and taken a look at them. He knew many of their faces. They were young, like him, and led by the older dragon riders. There were humans, elves, and orcs among them. One face was more recognizable than all of the other others—Dirklen. He was a sour-faced youth, with fair hair and skin like Dyphestive, and they had never gotten along.

Shamrok led him into his quarters, which was little more than four walls, a cot and blanket, and no door. "You can wash if you want to in the bathhouse. Help yourself in the galley." He poked the finger of his dragon gauntlet in Dyphestive's chest. "Don't overdo it!"

"Then what?"

"You have to ask?" Shamrok gave him a comical smile. "Rest. You'll need it." He marched out of the barracks and was soon out of sight.

Dyphestive ran for the galley. Rolls of hard bread and butter were on the table along with a pitcher of water and some wine, but not much else. He drank and ate heartily. It was the most he'd eaten in days. He ate every roll in the basket, fully expecting them to come back at any moment and yell at him. But it never happened.

He ambled over to the window and looked outside. No sign of the Doom Riders anywhere. An unsettling feeling that he couldn't explain crawled into his belly. *What are they up to?*

18

———

Drysis met with the Brothers of Destruction in a cove of rocks far from the barracks. Scar and Shamrok were sitting on adjacent boulders, tossing a dagger back and forth. Ghost was standing quietly off by himself.

"All three of you have spent time with Dyphestive. I need your assessment."

Ghost nodded at her.

"Oh, thank you for that," she said sarcastically. "Your input is as helpful as ever. Shamrok?"

"I like him." Shamrok snatched the dagger out of the air in a fluid motion and tossed it back. "I say we train him."

"You're only saying that because you don't want to walk up and down that hill again," Scar replied. He flicked the dagger back at Shamrok. "And I can't blame you. That's grueling, even without a coal-laden wheelbarrow."

Drysis stiffened. "I need a straight answer. We have to decide whether or not to keep him or end him."

"It would be a waste of a strong back," Shamrok added. "He seems pretty able to me. I see no reason why he can't learn to fight and hunt like us. He has all of the potential and then some, apparently."

"I say we kill him." Scar caught the dagger and tossed it into the ground. "I know what you are angling at, Drysis. You wonder if he's like a horse that can be broken. Well, I say this—he can't. He's been gone too long and breathed on his own too much."

Shamrok nodded. "Agreed. Not only that, but he's pushed that cart up the hill over a dozen times. I can't think of another youth that ever made it past the first day. They all begged for mercy. Even the tough ones. He climbs the hill like a stubborn mule."

"Aye, he's a glutton for punishment. I don't think he'll change," Scar added.

Drysis ground her teeth and paced. She had a relatively big decision to make in regard to Dyphestive. She'd been searching for him for three years, and she finally had him. But she'd gotten used to being out in the field. She wanted to ride with freedom in the wild steppes again as well as serve her master, Black Frost. "He's a strong candidate to be one of us. Stronger, perhaps, assuming that he's a natural. But he missed the age of ripening. His chance to be a

Risker has passed. It's the life of a foot soldier for him. Like us."

"Yeah," Shamrok said as he peered upward. "I rode a dragon once. Didn't last. The bloody thing bucked me like a bronco." He spit out black juice. "Fell so far I broke my leg when it happened. Stupid dragons."

"Aye," Scar replied. "Mine nearly bit my arm off. Then I got in trouble for trying to kill it. Who is more valuable? Me or a tail-wagging dragon."

"The dragon," Shamrok mused.

"Heh, right. "

The Doom Riders were a unique lot compared to ordinary soldiers. They weren't *naturals* but were still brought up to become Riskers. Many of the children washed out of the dragon-riding program, and washing out usually meant being killed or never heard from again.

It all started during an age of maturity called the ripening. It was the age when boys and girls turned from adolescents to young men and women. During that time, they were chosen to bond with the dragons. In some cases, the dragons would kill them. In others, they bonded. It wasn't an exact science, but the naturals, children born with apparent physical gifts, did better with it. But other youths, strong-willed and intelligent, could bond with dragons as well.

The Doom Riders, one and all, were such people. They were tough, fierce, and ready for a challenge. The problem was, the dragons didn't take to them. But they were savvy enough to escape the dragons' wrath. They were survivors who walked with a grudge and were naturally mean-spirited, making them formidable soldiers. And they did have another saving grace—the dragon horses, which were called gourn, liked them.

Shamrok rubbed his eye. "I say that we put him in the pit and see how he fares. Give it a few days. If that doesn't break him, nothing will."

"I'm telling you, that one won't be broken. He'll die first," Scar said. "Think about it. He has nothing to live for now that all of his friends are dead. He missed his chance to become a Risker. What is he really going to do? Become one of us? No, there is too much good in him for that to happen. He has pride. That's how he survives."

"Perhaps we should ease up on the youth," she said.

Scar gave her an incredulous look. "What? Make friends with him? Not me."

"You'll do what I say, won't you, Scar?" she said.

"Of course, but tell me, we aren't going to coddle him, are we?"

Shamrok raised his hand. "I'll play on the lighter side, and Scar can take the darker. How does that sound?"

With a frown, she nodded. "Let him rest well tonight. Tomorrow, put him in the pit, and we'll see how he fares after a few more days of that. If that doesn't break him, well"—she pointed her crossbow at Scar—"I guess we'll have to kill him." She pulled the trigger. The mechanism clicked, and the bolt fired into the boulder beside Scar's cheek.

Scar didn't bat an eye.

Drysis pumped her crossbow handle and rested the weapon against her shoulder. "You're dismissed."

19

The next step in Grey Cloak's journey took him south to Lake Flugen, where Gunder Island lay. Gunder Island was a range of mountains surrounded by forest and circling beaches. No boats or docks lined the shore. Men didn't like Gunder Island—giants did.

Grey Cloak marveled the first time he saw a giant. He was riding in the saddle, behind Anya, on Cinder's back when she pointed at the tree tops. Huge brutish men half as tall as the largest trees were walking through the forest and strolling along the beaches. At first, he did a double take, thinking that something was wrong with his eyes. That was when a giant dressed in animal skins chucked a rock bigger than Grey Cloak's head at Cinder.

"Not to worry. The giants are temperamental, but if they don't see you, they won't bother you. And no ships come here. The lake giants destroy them. But we are on good terms with most of them. For now."

"Good to know."

Cinder landed inside the mouth of a dormant volcano. The tremendous crater was rich in flora and wildlife. The walls of the crater had various levels of natural shelving. Many caves were exceptionally large and others, small. Dragons poked their heads out of those caves, but the flying reptiles' numbers weren't many.

Justus was the first to dismount his dragon, Firestok, whom he'd introduced Grey Cloak to earlier. He waved them over. "Come with me. I think these dragons would like some dragon time, if you know what I mean."

Grey Cloak shook his head. "I don't think I want to know what you mean."

Justus chuckled as he made his way through the woodland trail. The plants and trees were colorful, and flocks of brightly colored hummingbirds buzzed by. "We call this place Hidemark. It's our sanctuary. Black Frost would never think to look for us here. He hates the giants, and the giants hate him. Thankfully, we have an agreement that allows us to stay here."

"And what might that be?" Grey Cloak asked.

"That we kill Black Frost."

"Why don't the giants kill Black Frost?"

"A good question." Justus kept walking down the path.

Grey Cloak gave Anya a funny look, and she shrugged at him.

Staying on Justus's footsteps, he said, "Well?"

"Well what?"

"Why don't the giants fight Black Frost?"

"You would have to ask them. But in my opinion, they have a silent agreement. Black Frost leaves them alone, and they leave Black Frost alone. The giants are a guarded race. There aren't that many. They won't fight if they don't have to. But deep in my gut, I think there is another underlying reason."

"What is that?"

"They're lazy." Justus pointed. "Almost there."

Just ahead was a fortress built against the crater wall. It was over five stories tall but looked small compared to the crater. Stone columns wrapped in natural vine guarded the entrance like a temple. A flight of many steps led up to the fortress and inside. From a distance, the normal naked eye wouldn't notice the fortress, as it blended in very well with nature.

"This is it. Hidemark, home of the Lords of the Air."

Grey Cloak arched an eyebrow and followed Justus up the steps with Anya in tow. The inside of Hidemark didn't reveal anything extraordinary. All of the walls were chiseled stone from work that could have been done eons ago. Torches were fastened to iron brackets on the wall. Barrel-sized stone urns were burning on the floor. The chamber was deep, with a row of inner columns stretching as far as the eye could see.

"The giants occupied this place long ago. That's why all of the proportions are so enormous. Fortunately for us, it's a fitting space for dragons too," Justus said as he walked deeper into the fortress. Between the rows of columns were oversized alcoves and huge pieces of furniture made of stone. A horse-sized dragon with pitch-black scales was lying in a stone chair like a cat. Its tail was hanging down, and its eyelids peeked open. "That's Snaggle. Don't ever sit in his chair."

"Understood."

Justus veered into an alcove on the left. A huge mural of a map of Gapoli was painted on the wall, and several individuals were standing beside it. "This is the map room, or the war room, which we sometimes call it, and these individuals are the Lords of the Air. Or at least, what is left of them."

There were three elves, an orc, one dwarf, a lizard man, and a gnome. All of them were suited the same as Justus and Anya. Their armor had a dull shine, and the weapons they were carrying had dragon-winged pommels. Each of them was notable in one way or another. The elves were one man with a narrow face and a strong chin and two gorgeous women in armor; the orc was a shaggy-haired brute; the dwarf's beard was as black as charcoal, his face as square as a lantern, and he had a big belly; and the lizard man's eyes shone like diamonds. That left the gnome, who was the most incongruous and had the appearance of a pudgy little woman with a pleasant smile on her wizened face.

Grey Cloak nodded and said, "Hello." An awkward feeling crept over him. He felt out of place. The Sky Riders, also known as the Lords of the Air, were a formidable lot, brimming with great confidence. They looked him over like he was a sow put up for auction.

The dwarf broke the silence with a gruff statement. "I thought there were two of them."

"It is good to see you too, Hammerjaw," Anya said. "Dyphestive, son of Olgstern Stronghair, has been taken captive by Black Frost. At the moment, we have more pressing matters at hand. But first, we'll start with introductions."

20

Anya gestured toward the only other male elf in the room. He was handsome, light haired, and middle-aged. "This is Arik. The twins beside him are his younger sisters, Stayzie and Mayzie." The sisters were enchanting, with honey-blond hair flowing over their shoulders.

"Well met," the sisters said as one.

The orc stretched out his powerful arm. He was the largest person in the room, and his head was very big. "I'm Hogrim." He crushed Grey Cloak's hand in his grip. "Welcome, son of Zanna Paydark."

Grey Cloak grimaced and pulled his hand free, nodding.

"This is Fomander," Anya said as she pointed at the lizard man, whose steely gaze shone brightly. His arms were crossed, and he nodded.

"And last but not least, even though she is the smallest, is Yuri Gnomeknower."

The gnome had a twinkle in her eyes and spoke with peppy energy. "Pleased to meet you." She gazed up at Anya. "He's cute. Have you laid claim on him?"

Anya's cheeks flushed, but she recovered with a disgusted look and said, "Don't be silly."

Yuri shrugged. "That's good to know. I like to know."

"Yes, well, now you know," Anya said. She turned her attention to Justus and raised her eyebrows.

Justus nodded then put his hand on Grey Cloak's shoulder and said, "I know that it is going to take some time to get acquainted, and we can do more of that later, but for now, we need to discuss our situation." He ran his gaze over the group. "If I can have your attention, we need to bring Grey Cloak up to speed."

"Why is he named after a garment?" Mayzie asked.

"Yes, why is that?" Stayzie added. "I thought his name was Dindae."

Yuri rubbed his cloak in her fingers. "This is a very interesting fabric. Where did you get it?"

"We don't have time for another one of your long meetings, Justus," Hammerjaw said. "He needs to be trained now. We need soldiers, not historians."

"Agreed." Hogrim jabbed a finger at Grey Cloak. "He needs weapons, and he needs a dragon. The sooner he is in the air, the better."

All of a sudden, everyone started talking at once. Talking turned into squabbling, then squabbling turned into arguing.

"He needs training!"

"We need to attack Black Frost now!"

"How can we fight Black Frost without an army? He has hundreds of Riskers, and there's not even ten of us!"

"I want to know what we are eating. I'm hungry!"

Grey Cloak shrank away from the blustering brood. *Zooks! They really have issues. It's no wonder they are losing.* He made his way over to the map and studied it. It spanned from wall to wall and was intricately painted. He stood in front of the area that was marked The Shelf. Just above his head was Lake Flugen and Gunder Island, where he was currently located. All the way near the top of the ceiling was Dark Mountain. Suddenly, Dyphestive seemed very far away. *Oh no!*

In the back of his mind, Grey Cloak always had a plan. His current one was slipping away from the Sky Riders the first chance that he got. With his gaze scouring the map, he realized something. He was surrounded by a huge body of water, and he hadn't seen any boats when they flew in. It appeared there was only one way in and one way out. *I'll need a dragon.*

Justus threw his arms up. "All right! All right! Can we have a complete conversation without breaking into the same tired arguments? Everyone stifle it!"

The group fell silent.

"Thank you." Justus nodded and caught his breath. "We have a new member, and he needs to be briefed. Grey Cloak, I'm sure that you feel overwhelmed by this, so if you will be patient, I'll bring you up to speed." He scanned the others' faces. "And without interruption."

Hammerjaw opened his mouth, but Justus's hard look made him close it again.

Justus moved over to the map and stood in front of it. "Decades ago, there was unity among the dragon riders. We were the sworn defenders of Gapoli, devoted to keeping the peace. All of this came about after the Dragon Wars, when the Wizards of the Watch and the dragons battled to near extinction. For centuries, the troubles were avoided. Certainly, there were wars and skirmishes in the lands, but nothing that would destroy all of civilization.

"But gradually, a festering evil grew in the north. Black Frost. He was a dragon, much like Cinder or Firestok, but with very strong powers of persuasion. You see, like his forefathers who were slain, he felt his kind was the superior race. And he did not care to share dominion, though he continued to aid the Sky Riders as the guardians of the world.

"Then came the great betrayal. Black Frost grew in size and strength as well as in ambition. He secretly turned more Sky Riders to his cause and called them Riskers." He pointed up at Dark Mountain, and his voice took on a darker tone. "In those black crests came the Day of Betrayal. Black Frost gathered all of the Sky Riders and announced his supremacy. He ordered them to pledge their loyalty. To the shock and dismay of many, over half of the Sky Riders pledged their allegiance. His words were clear. 'Join me or die.' Over fifty joined. Twenty-five resisted. Black Frost ordered their immediate execution. Only twenty survived that ferocious battle and escaped. You are looking at what is left of them, aside from Anya. The rest have been slaughtered by Black Frost's growing army of Riskers over the years."

Hogrim grunted and punched his fist into his hand. "Black Frost must die."

"And he will die," Fomander said. His tongue flicked out of his mouth, and he pulled his sword and raised it over his head. The rest of the Sky Riders did the same. "He will die by our hands."

In unison, the group said, "Vengeance for all! Death to Black Frost!"

21

____

Even though Grey Cloak felt moved by their cause, he couldn't help but say, "I sympathize with your circumstances, but what does all of this have to do with me?"

The Lords of the Air put away their weapons and stared at him with funny looks.

Anya stepped beside him and said, "You'll have to forgive him, but Grey Cloak only recently learned that Zanna Paydark was his mother. He doesn't know about all of this. It's new to him."

"Well, sort of new. I did live in Dark Mountain, and I've seen the Riskers and their dragons."

Hammerjaw stepped forward and asked, "You've had eyes in the dark belly—how many Riskers have you seen?"

"There are over one hundred dragons in the kennels and well over one hundred riders."

"Over one hundred!" Hammerjaw slapped his head. "Black Frost's army grows, and our army shrinks. This is preposterous, Justus. We must act!"

"Don't start the arguments again, please," Justus said. "We have been well aware that Black Frost's army is growing. And that is why we are gathered here. To duplicate his efforts." He eyed Grey Cloak. "Starting with you and by recruiting others, we plan to rebuild the ranks of the Sky Riders. And we will rebuild them here. In Hidemark."

"So this is it so far?" Grey Cloak's gaze slid over the members of the group. "Black Frost also has armies that boast tens of thousands in numbers. It will take decades to build an army to match his. And frankly, I don't see the concern. There aren't any wars going on that I know of. Back in Havenstock, we lived peacefully. In my mind, all was in order."

"I can't believe my ears," Arik said. "How can you be the son of Zanna Paydark? She died in Black Frost's grip. She died giving her life to save ours, and you shrug that off?"

"Preposterous!" Hammerjaw said.

Grey Cloak suddenly wanted to hide inside his cloak. He felt ashamed, but it was so hard to love a mother he'd never known. He'd given up thinking about his parents long ago. As far as he knew, he'd never had any. "She might have been your friend, but I've never known my mother...

or my father, for the matter." He turned his back and ran away.

"Look at that! He runs," Hogrim said. "He is not fit to be a Sky Rider."

"No, but he sure can run," Mayzie commented.

Once Grey Cloak had made it out of earshot, he raced into the daylight and wiped the tears from his eyes. He didn't understand what was expected of him, and he didn't want any part in the war that had killed the mother he'd never known. With his head down, he walked into the forest.

What do they want with me? Why can't they leave me alone?

Buried in his thoughts, he walked right up on Cinder and Firestok without noticing them. He started to turn around, but it was too late. They saw him.

"Where are you going, Grey Cloak? You just got here," Cinder said. He was lying on the ground beside Firestok. Their tails were intertwined behind them. "Go back inside."

"Can't you see that the elf is upset?" Firestok asked. "His eyes are wet."

"No, they aren't." Grey Cloak pinched his eyes. "I'll leave you alone."

"Stay and talk with us, Grey Cloak. I want to know what is on your mind," Firestok said. She had a very soothing voice.

"Ah, they are all rambling on about my mother and killing Black Frost. I don't know a mother. I never had a mother. Or father. I don't know these things, and they act like I ought to."

Firestok nodded. "I see. Well, how about I talk and you listen."

"You sound like Justus." When her eyes grew wide, he said, "But much sweeter." He let out a sigh. "I'll listen, but try not to bore me like they did."

"I'll make it brief. After all, if anyone knows how long-winded Justus can be, it's me." She uncoiled her tail from Cinder's and laid it in front of her on the ground. "Have a seat."

"I thought you said it wouldn't take very long," Grey Cloak said as he sat down.

"It won't. At least, not for a dragon. Now, about your mother, Zanna. She and Olgstern Stronghair were the leaders of the Sky Riders and were present at the Day of Betrayal. They were very close friends as well, brave and wise. It was their valiant efforts that allowed the remnants of the Sky Riders to escape. You see, they foresaw that Black Frost was up to something, so they weren't taken completely by surprise, and the two of them sacrificed themselves to buy time. The Sky Riders revere them, for if it weren't for them, Black Frost would have won already. Zanna and Olgstern bought time for not only the Sky Riders but also for the rest of the world."

"Frankly, I don't see anything happening that is that bad," Grey Cloak said.

"No, but you still ran, didn't you?" Firestok replied. "And why is that? Because you want to be free. Right?"

He nodded.

"On the surface," Firestok said, "the people don't see the secret war that is being waged between the Sky Riders and the Riskers. After all, they are more concerned with their own busy lives, but they are completely oblivious to the heroes who protect them—the Sky Riders, the dragons, and the Wizards of the Watch, along with many other heroes, like you, who are working for the greater good in the background.

"But don't think for a moment that a storm isn't coming. And I believe that you can already feel it in your bones. The world is full of agitation, and the people are distracted by the war in the air, not the war outside their front doors. Perhaps you are too young to see it clearly, but with age will come vision. Be patient. In the meantime, trust us."

Firestok's words rang true, but he didn't want to admit it. He didn't like being trapped on an island and twenty days away from Dyphestive. Knowing that he was out there was killing him.

"But I can't leave Dyphestive, out there, with them. I need to bring him back. He needs me."

"You're going to have to have faith, Grey Cloak. Have

faith in us, and have faith in your friend. After all, he is the son of Olgstern Stronghair."

He combed his hair behind his ear and said, "About that... how did we come to grow up in Dark Mountain?"

"The answer to that is simple but unpleasant. After Black Frost killed the rebelling Sky Riders, he went after their families. Not only did he go after them, but he had his soldiers already positioned at their homes." Her voice became sorrowful. "He killed the husbands and the wives of the Sky Riders and kidnapped all of the surviving children like you."

22

DARK MOUNTAIN

Shamrok and Scar escorted Dyphestive into a cavern in the mountainside. Both men walked behind him, carrying torches.

Scar kept shoving him forward. "Hurry up."

He picked up the pace, even though he didn't know where he was going. It was pitch-black in all directions, and dampness hung in the air. Fifty yards into the cavern, he came upon a set of wide stairs that had been crudely hewn out of the stone. He ventured down the winding stairwell.

"You're going to like this, boy," Scar said. "The Pit is where we finally get rid of you."

Shamrok let out a hoarse chuckle. "Yeah, but you'll make plenty of new friends down here. Hungry ones."

Dyphestive swallowed the lump in his throat. Judging by their voices, which were dripping with sarcasm, he realized that it might be the end. His jaw tightened, and all he wanted to do was turn around and run. Only his burning hatred for them kept his rising fear in check. *I won't give them the satisfaction.*

After going over ten stair levels and switching back and forth, they came to a stop on a landing at the bottom in front of a solid iron door. It was sealed shut by a metal drop bar.

Shamrok put his ear to the door and gave a goofy grin. "Hmm... I think something hungry is in there. Yes, it's been a long time since the snake has been fed."

"Snake? I thought it was a wolf spider," Scar replied.

"Oh, I think they like to fight over their meals, and it's been a long time since we fed them. Those spiders bind a body up in those silky fibers and feed on the blood later. They turn bodies into living canteens." Shamrok made a sour face and shivered. "I saw one eating a man once. The boy was still alive." He put a heavy hand on Dyphestive's shoulder. "A boy just like you. Grisly."

"Aye, a spider can feed on a boy like him for days." Scar lifted the drop bar from the door and set it aside.

Dyphestive's skin turned clammy. He didn't care for tight places, let alone dark pits with snakes and spiders.

Scar held a torch in his face and said, "You're getting pale, boy. Are you getting scared? You should be." He fished a white candle stem out of his clothing. It was only a couple of inches long. He lit it with his torch. "Take this.

But once that candle goes out, well, you'll be in the black forever."

Dyphestive took the candle in his trembling fingers. "How long do I have to stay in there?"

"The question isn't how long you *have* to stay in there. It's how long *can* you stay in there." Scar grabbed the door handle and pulled the door open. The corroded hinges creaked loudly. "Get in."

A musty, sour smell wafted out of the pitch-black opening. Dyphestive's nose twitched. The smell was awful. He thrust the candle out in front of him with meager effort.

Scar gave him a hard shove in the back. "Get in there!"

He stumbled into the black cave and fought to keep his footing.

"Don't let the snakes and spiders get you," Shamrok said as Scar slammed the door shut.

The drop bar was set back into place with a clank. *I hate them.*

Dyphestive didn't hear anything else after that except for his breath and the soft crackle of the candle's wick burning. He held the candle out before him. The pit was nothing more than a cave that had been made into a ten-foot-by-ten-foot cell. It didn't even have a cot or a bed of rotting hay or a blanket, only scraps of gnawed clothing and bits and pieces of bone. The walls were crudely hewn, and many small holes had been bored into the rock.

It was cold, and the walls and the floor were slick from

dripping cave water. Dyphestive eyed the flame of his candle. The white wax was running over his fingers. It wouldn't be long before it went out. He found a spot against the wall that appeared to be dryer than the rest of the hole and squatted.

Scar and Shamrok had led on that the pit was a huge catacomb filled with giant snakes and spiders. They were liars. All they'd wanted to do was scare him. *I won't let them win. I'll stay in here forever first.*

He sulked, contemplating all that had happened with Grey Cloak and Talon. Only one thing came to mind—he would make the Doom Riders pay, somehow, some way. *I'm going to bust them up.*

The candle had melted to a nub. Dyphestive set it on the floor and watched the last of the small flame flicker. He missed the campfires with Talon and the star-filled sky in Havenstock. Everything that he knew and loved was gone. The candle flame was all he had. It fluttered and spit. The pool of wax beneath it shone with the flame's final reflection. Then flame turned blue and died. The world went black. Dyphestive sank his head into his chest and sighed. Something crawled over his fingers. *Get me out of here!*

23

The sounds of tiny feet could be heard crawling inside the small holes that perforated Dyphestive's cage. Whatever had crawled over his fingers had come and gone, but something else was coming. In his mind, he could see spiders, small snakes, and insects making their way through the holes, coming to feast on his body.

His jaw clenched. *No, I won't give in!* He set it in his mind that Scar and Shamrok only wanted to scare him. *This is a game. That's all it is.*

Something dropped into his hair. He raked it away and squished it in his hand with a crunch then wiped his palm on the wet floor. "Yuck."

Dyphestive missed his fire. He needed the flame. He had nothing but the sound of his heart beating. *Thump-thump. Thump-thump. Thump-thump.* Though he was trying to stay calm, his breathing became labored. He felt invisible fingers all over him and brushed them away. Each and every hair on his body was standing on end. His mind was gripped with terror. *I will make them pay!*

The minutes were long, and he lost track of time. Whenever he felt something, he would brush or slap it off. Sometimes he would grab at something on his body and come up with nothing. Other times, it felt like he was crushing bugs or spiders. He flicked at his ears and swatted wildly at the air.

The longer he sat in the dark, the more touching, probing, and crawling he felt. He curled up in a ball and tried to ignore it or pretend that it wasn't there. Jaw clenching, he rocked back and forth. *It's all a dream. It's all a dream. This isn't real. It's all a dream.*

Things crawled through his hair, over his arms, and down his legs. He stuck his fingers in his ears. Something tried to crawl between his lips, and he spit it out. "Blecht!"

As time moved slowly on, Dyphestive was overwhelmed by the creepy and crawly things and started brushing away the creatures in a panic. He rose and searched the walls with his hands, looking for the door. He felt what he envisioned were spiders and insects crawling between his fingers and down his arms. The creatures swarmed up his feet and over his ankles and climbed higher up his leg. His hands touched the cold metal surface of the door, and he started beating it with his fists. "Let me out! Let me out!" He lowered his shoulder and rammed the door. "Let me out!"

Scar and Shamrok were sitting on the steps outside of the door, frowning. They were sharing a horn of ale that Shamrok often carried and chewing on hunks of dried meat.

"For the love of gravy, when is that boy going to try to claw his way out of there? It's been hours," Scar said as he took a swig of ale.

Shamrok chewed his food and swallowed then beckoned for the horn. "No one's ever lasted more than an hour, that I know of. Huh. He might be young, but he ain't no boy. Hardheaded, that one."

Dyphestive's muffled pleas erupted on the other side of the door.

"Speak of the dragon." Scar stood up. "It's about time."

Wham! Wham! Wham!

"He hits hard, that one," Scar commented as he sauntered to the door.

"You would know," Shamrok said as he stood and licked his salty fingers. Then he capped his horn of ale.

Scar put his face to the door and shouted, "Say, boy, are you ready to come out now? Are the bugs scaring you? Hah!"

Boom! The door rattled on its hinges. Scar jumped back.

Shamrok laughed. "Looks to me like the bugs are scaring you."

Boom! The door flexed outward, and the metal drop bar bent against the brackets.

With widening eyes, Shamrok exchanged concerned looks with Scar and commented, "Sweet onions, that boy's really getting a run at it, ain't he?"

Boom! The door buckled but didn't give. *Boom!*

"Get him out of there, Scar!" Shamrok ordered. "He's gonna bust it."

"He won't bust that." Scar hooked his fingers underneath the drop bar and lifted upward. But the bent bar was jammed in the brackets. "Cripes!"

Boom!

"Settle your horseshoes!" Scar roared. "He's like a mule kicking in there." He ripped the drop bar free and swung open the door.

Dyphestive charged through the gap with the whites of his eyes showing like moons. When

Shamrok stuck out his foot and tripped him, he stumbled into the stairs and immediately tried to crawl up them. Hundreds of assorted insects and spiders—bigger than a man's hands in some cases—were all over him. When their brittle and fuzzy bodies caught the wavering torchlight, they skittered away.

Scar grabbed Dyphestive's collar and threw him down

then turned his head toward the pit. When he stuck his torch into the chamber, thousands of spiders, centipedes, and tiny snakes scurried back into the holes, away from the torchlight. In a moment, all of them vanished. "If you don't want to go in there again, you'd better behave yourself. If not, I'll let those bugs crawl into your body and eat you from the inside out."

Sweat had drenched Dyphestive's broad, heaving chest.

Shamrok closed the door then picked up the metal locking bar and draped it over his shoulders. His freckled face reddened, and the muscles in his arms flexed. He groaned as he bent the thick bar straight and dropped it into the bracket, then he lowered his gaze on Dyphestive and said, "He's as white as a sheet. I think he got the message."

Scar lifted Dyphestive by his hair. "Get up." He shoved him toward the stairs. "Get going. The fun is just beginning."

24

HIDEMARK

I t was the wee hours of the morning, and a thin layer of fog had blanketed the forest floor. Grey Cloak had been up since before first light, running drills with the Sky Riders, a routine that had lasted for months. Hogrim of Hammerjaw would wake him up out of a dead sleep—because he would be exhausted from the day before—and he would eat a handful of fruit and nuts and wash it down with milk from the sap weeds. Then he would run for leagues, inside the crater of Gunder Island's exotic trails. Now, he was running with a spear hoisted over his head, following the elven sisters Mayzie and Stayzie.

He picked up the pace and caught up with the tireless tandem. They were no longer dressed in full armor. Instead, they'd substituted the heavier gear for more suitable forest-green cotton outfits that showed off their long legs and slender arms. Their hair was tied in ponytails that streamed behind their backs.

"We do an awful lot of running, and I think I've mastered it," he said.

The twins shared glances and picked up the pace. They knifed underneath the low-hanging branches and plunged their way into the leafy terrain of the forest.

Grey Cloak sped after them. Running behind them wasn't a problem. He had no trouble keeping pace. The problem was running with a spear raised over his head. His arms and shoulders burned from the effort. After jumping over a bed of ferns, he pushed through a waterfall of vines hanging in his path. He ran sideways so he could angle the spear through the net, and when he emerged on the other side of the vines, the twins were gone.

He stuck the spear in the ground. "Zooks."

The sisters were crafty. If he took his eyes off of them for a moment, they vanished. They'd been doing the drill with him all week long, and he'd lost them every time.

Grey Cloak rolled his shoulder and massaged it with his fingers. "Here we go again." He wiped the sweat off of his brow and scanned the woodland. Hoping to hear their soft footfalls, he closed his eyes. A breeze rustled the leaves. Birds chirped in the branches. Creek water trickled nearby.

Something was out of the ordinary. He felt eyes on him. When he opened his eyes, he looked from side to side, searching the tree branches. Then he picked up his spear and walked forward.

The fog at his feet covered their tracks, and they didn't leave much of a track to begin with. The terrain would swallow the footprints up like sand by a river bank. His eyes slid from side to side. *Come on, I know you are watching me. I can feel it.*

Grey Cloak caught a glimpse of a pair of eyes hidden behind a thicket. It was Mayzie. He pretended not to see her and walked on. *I have you now.*

He flipped his spear around. The tip of it was wooden and dull and only used for sparring. The shaft had indentations all over it from weeks of practice. He thrust the spear into the thicket. "Ah-ha!"

But Mayzie was gone. He poked his spear in the thicket again but found no sign of the elf woman. "Where in the world?"

"Looking for me?"

He whirled around and came face-to-face with Mayzie. "How'd you do that?"

"You have a blind spot," she said.

"No, I don't."

"Yes, you do," Stayzie said. She'd snuck in behind him. "Lords of Lightning, a hungry bear could have crept up on you." She shook her head and gave him a disappointed look. "That's a severe weakness."

Grey Cloak didn't understand it. He had heightened

senses and could hear a ladybug crawling on a leaf, but the elven women continued to get the drop on him. Even Zora did. He didn't understand it. "I let you sneak up on me. Try it again. I was only fooling."

Mayzie shook her head. "It would be one thing if you were improving, but you aren't. I'll have to report this to Justus. He'll be disappointed. Again."

"Great. More work for me," he said with a sigh. "I don't think it's fair to say I'm not improving. I'm better at everything you've taught me. I can fight with every weapon you've put in my hands. I've mastered the obstacles. I've memorized the dragon lore that's been taught to me. You can't expect me to be perfect at everything. So what if you slipped up on me. I'll get better."

Stayzie pulled a dagger from the sheath on her hip. "If we were the enemy, you would have been dead by now. You have a blind spot." She tossed the dagger up and caught it. "It can be fatal, not only for you but also for us."

Grey Cloak clenched his jaw. The Sky Riders had been working his fingers to the bone week after week. Nothing was ever good enough. He'd mastered bladed weapons, but Hogrim the orc said he needed to get better. His hands were thick with calluses, and he had bruises all over. Hammerjaw had made him lift wheels of stone that broke his back. The dwarf had told him to get stronger and work harder. The burly taskmaster could have been Rhonna's father. Fomander had trained him with bows, arrows, and throwing weapons. The lizard man's slit eyes always showed disappointment. Yuri Gnomeknower had made him cook, and he'd prepared the evening meals for everybody. Late into the night, he would clean everything from the pots and pans to the racks of weapons. They'd bested him over and over again, but he never saw any evidence that any of them were that much better than he was. So far as he was concerned, he was just as good as they were.

"I'll tell you what." He shoved his spear at Mayzie's chest. "How about I hide and you seek? Let's see how that turns out."

Mayzie spun the spear around in her hands slowly and looked at her sister. Stayzie nodded.

"Agreed," the said together.

He smiled and said, "Catch me if you can," and raced into the woodland.

25

For the first time, Grey Cloak finally had a chance to prove himself. If there was one thing that he prided himself on, it was running. No one could catch him, especially if he had a lead.

Over the grueling weeks of training, he'd come to know the forest jungle like the back of his hand, and he darted between the trees and leapt over the shrubbery like a stag. He stretched his legs farther and farther, putting as much distance between him and the twins as he could. In truth, he didn't despise getting caught by the likes of Mayzie and Stayzie. They were captivating. But his zeal to beat them outweighed his attraction to them for the moment.

Grey Cloak knew exactly where he wanted to lead them. A place where they would never expect him to go— the marsh. This time, he was going to get them.

He sped up a mosslike hill and slid on his boots down the other side. He'd been doing a lot of running, but one thing hadn't happened. He'd never achieved the lightning speed he had before when they battled the Scourge. The sudden burst of speed had come out of nowhere, and he wasn't sure if it had come from him or the cloak. He didn't have the cloak now. They never let him use it during training. He missed the comfort and confidence it brought.

But that wasn't the only thing that was on his mind. Dyphestive was too. The Sky Riders had stonewalled him on any conversations about his blood brother. They wouldn't entertain any thoughts of rescuing Dyphestive, either. They wanted Grey Cloak focused on one thing and one thing only—destroying Black Frost. All of them were on the same page, but he wasn't. *I need to get off of this island and save my brother.*

The sulfur-like stink of wetlands caught his nose as he came upon a bed of fog the height of the cattail stalks. Certain that he had a large lead on the twins, he waded chest deep into the water. He moved quickly through the murk to the root base of a willow tree and climbed into the twisting branches, hid among the dangling leaves, and waited. *They're going to hate this.*

Grey Cloak sat in the branches, alone with his thoughts, watching for their approach. He hated the idea of waiting a year to find Dyphestive. Every day, he tried to think of new ways to get off Gunder Island, but the Sky

Riders watched him like a hawk. He tried to play along to get along, but he didn't like it.

Mayzie and Stayzie appeared on the edge of the marsh, turning their noses up and away from the stagnant water.

Stayzie used the spear-like staff and entered the water. She had a deep frown on her face and beckoned her sister. "Come on."

Grey Cloak stifled a laugh. Even if the brooding sisters caught him, it was still worth it to see them covered in grime, with snarls on their faces. They'd all tormented and overtrained him, and it was time for him to get some revenge.

They passed under him and didn't look up once, then they moved beyond the great willow.

He slithered down the tree like a snake and slipped right into the water behind them. The women's heads twisted from side to side. Never once did they look back.

He crept back up on both of them. *Now I have you.*

The fog thickened suddenly, and he lost sight of both women. When the fog thinned, the twins, who had been right in front of him a moment earlier, were gone. *No!*

He squinted and spun in a slow circle. They had vanished like ghosts. *No, no, no, no, no, no! They must be close. They must be!*

Something smacked him on the back of the head. *Crack!*

He spun around and rubbed the knot popping up on his head. The twins stood before him, grinning.

Grey Cloak's shoulders sagged. "I'm not even going to ask."

"Well, you should ask," Stayzie said.

"I *have* asked." He slapped the water. "You've never told me!"

Stayzie throttled his head again with the spear.

"Ow! Quit doing that."

"Your problem is that you rely on your senses too much. The eyes, the ears, even the heart will fool you," Stayzie said.

"What does that even mean?"

Stayzie handed him the staff. "It means what it means. Hopefully, you'll figure it out." She slung the muck off of her hands. "I'm all dirty for nothing. How disappointing."

The twins walked out of the marsh and left Grey Cloak behind.

26

"One would think that at the end of the day, I might have some time to myself," Grey Cloak said. He was standing inside a kitchen galley in front of a wood-burning stove. Hidemark had all of the necessities of modern living, which included everything from herbs and spices, most of which were locally grown, to ancient bottles of wine. He used a wooden spoon to stir the contents of a metal pot. "I mean, I've done every task that's been asked of me and without complaint."

Yuri Gnomeknower huffed. The fuzzy-faced little woman was wearing an ivory kitchen apron and no armor, sitting on a stool with her long nose deep in a book. "You're complaining now."

"Barely." Even though his limbs were weary, he couldn't help but smile. He liked Yuri. She wasn't as intense as the rest of them. It had been another day of backbreaking training. He'd spent most of the day in the weapons room, battling with Fomander and Hogrim. They never made it easy on him, and he had bruises and scabs to show for it.

From small spice jars, he added more gingerroot and bane's breath to his pot. The aroma was strong but good. It tickled his nose. "Isn't it late to be cooking? Everyone has eaten."

"We aren't cooking food." She pointed a stubby finger at him. "Follow the recipe."

He yawned. "Of course." His clean fingers ran down the length of a piece of parchment that Yuri had given him. It had a long list of ingredients and different measurements. He moved back and forth to the stone shelving and plucked out small jars one by one.

"Eye of lizard. Feather of sparrow. Ground tiger ash. Smoked buttercrisp. Bloodworm. Mandrake moon. Godard slime." He sniffed the last one. "*Uck.* I'm glad this isn't a recipe." He tossed the ingredients into the boiling pot according to their proper order and stirred. It made a sweet aroma at first, but after several minutes, it stank. "Oh my, that's awful."

"Good." Yuri closed her book and tossed it onto the prep table then stood on the stool. "It should be ready. What is the next step?"

Grey Cloak ran his finger down the page. "Um...

remove from the fire, let it cool, and drink." He gave her a horrified look. "Drink?"

She showed him a smile full of whimsy. "That's what it says."

"Me or you?"

"You."

"This sounds more like something that a gnome would drink, not an elf. Are you certain?"

"I'm always certain."

With a grunt, Grey Cloak sat the pot on the table. He couldn't help but think that everything he was doing, he was doing for their amusement. *This is getting really tiresome.*

"Keep stirring. It will go down smoother." Yuri jumped from the stool to the table. Even though she was little more than three feet tall, she was taller than Grey Cloak up there. She grabbed a ladle from the rack that hung over the table and tapped it in the palm of her hand then peered into the pot. "It looks very good. Your touch with the ingredients is a gift. Not many have it."

"This is hardly a challenge. All I am doing is following the instructions."

"Precisely. Many can't, but there is more to this than just that. Keep stirring."

He did as she asked. The contents of the pot were a swirl of cotton white and inky black. The aroma changed from the stink of mud to peppermint, to cinnamon, and back to peppermint. Suddenly, the concoction began to sparkle. The dull colors transformed into bright shades of green and yellow. He couldn't hide his surprise. "Whoa. What just happened?"

Yuri dipped the ladle into the pot, which came up higher than her knees. She lifted the sparkling concoction to his lips. With a twinkle in her eye, she said, "Drink."

He pulled his chin away. "That? Why?"

"Stop asking so many questions. You made it." She wiggled her fingers. "Open wide."

"But—"

Before he could get out another word, his mouth was opened wide by a power that was not his. It felt like a giant's hands had locked on his head and pried his mouth open. He couldn't move a muscle.

Yuri poured the concoction down his throat. It burned like the strongest peppermint. "The time has come for your awakening."

His eyes followed her as she set the ladle inside the pot. She shoved the pot away and sat cross-legged before him then wagged her finger and said, "Now that I have you, it is time to listen. There is magic in *all* of us. You must learn to use it. Watch."

Grey Cloak's body warmed up from the inside out with a tingling sensation that burned all over inside. It didn't hurt, but it was as if he could feel every part of himself at once. All of the aches and pains went away. He felt more alive than he'd ever felt before. *What is happening to me? What did she do?*

"You must learn to trust me, Grey Cloak. Trust all of us." She spread her small hands out. A mystic rose of energy appeared between them. She balled up her fists, and the rose hardened and shimmered with angry light. When the gnome spread out her fingers, the ball of energy transformed into a web made from lightning that lit up her face. "This power is your power. It is within. Do you wish to harness it?"

The invisible hands that were holding him fast eased. He barely managed to nod and say, "Yes."

"Good." The fire in her hands went out. "The training will begin tomorrow."

27

Sweat dripped down Grey Cloak's cheek. His shoulders trembled. Inside the palms of his hands was mystic webbing, and inside the webbing was a hunk of stone as big as his head. He was standing in one of Hidemark's enormous alcoves with Yuri watching him.

"Good. Good," she said. "Concentrate. Hold it longer."

His arms shook. The magic between his fingers faded, and the rock dropped onto the floor and chipped. He gasped. "Zooks," he said, panting. "Do you have to keep making the stones bigger? I would like to master the smaller ones first."

"You can hold the smaller ones. It's the bigger ones that you must master."

"Can I get a drink? I feel like I've been fighting with Hammerjaw and Hogrim all day."

When she nodded, he grabbed a canteen that was lying on the floor nearby. Using magic wasn't nearly as easy as he'd hoped. They'd been training for weeks, and he'd only mastered the rudiments. He drank deeply and gulped down most of what was in the canteen then replaced its cap and swung it around. "So Sky Riders are wizards too?"

"Hah. No," Yuri said in a matter-of-fact manner. "Wizards weave magic with greater precision. They create spells and potions and record them on scrolls. Our magic is a different discipline that we are born with. We pull energy from the same source, but that source is connected to us, and it's limited."

"What do you mean? Can't we draw as much as we want?"

"Not without destroying ourselves. We should only use it when needed. Use it too much, and the magic will pervert us." Yuri pushed up her sleeves. Her forearms were black with scars and burn marks.

"Oh my, the magic did that?"

"Magic is not a part of flesh and bone. That is why we place it in inanimate objects, such as wands, staffs, swords, and stones. Those items don't have living bodies, but we do. That is why most of the Sky Riders don't practice it. It's too unpredictable, and"—she lifted a finger—"one can become addicted to it. Like I did. As you can see, it cost me dearly."

"You look well enough, aside from your arms being charred."

"Yes, but I can barely swing my sword. What I've taught you is just enough to get you out of a bind. But as of this day forward, I'll teach you no more. You know enough to learn on your own."

"That's it?"

Yuri nodded. "That's it. I'll practice with you, but I won't allow you to become like me. It's too risky." She eyed him. "Besides, you don't really want to master wizardry, do you?"

"I like it, but truthfully, I never wanted to master any of this. I'm only doing it because you aren't giving me any choice." Grey Cloak stole over to the alcove entrance and peered down the hallway. No one was in the master chamber. He went back into the alcove. "Yuri, don't you think that by now, I should have embraced this? I mean, I appreciate the time and energy that is being put into me to rebuild the Sky Riders, but I'm not feeling it." He started to pace and traced his finger along the chamber wall. "Shouldn't I feel something, like the rest of you?"

"You are very indifferent. I'll say that." She was bent over, lacing up her boots. "Blooming laces. No matter how much I lace them, they always come loose." She straightened her back and walked alongside him. "What do you feel?"

"I only worry about Dyphestive. I want to save him. I gave my word. I gave Talon my word."

"You can't help them now. You aren't ready. Be patient. Remember, you can see them after one year. Half of that has passed." She reached up and patted his back. "We shall see how it goes. You'll be better prepared by then. The same as we will."

He frowned and said, "Frankly, I feel like we are wasting time. I could be helping now. We all could." He tapped his fist on his stomach. "I can't shake the gnawing in my gut. Have you ever felt that? Like something you are doing is wrong? Like you are losing something?"

"What we are doing isn't wrong, I assure you. It's right, I promise. Trust me. Trust us."

"I do." *But not entirely. Why, I don't know.*

"Come, let's practice your spell casting." She broke away and moved to the center of the room then spread her arms out wide over her head and fanned them back and forth. A sphere of red energy appeared between her palms. "Prepare yourself."

Grey Cloak nodded. Ever since he'd drunk the concoction weeks ago, he'd felt a special fire burning within. From there, he could call forth the mystic powers of wizardry. The fire slid from his belly, up his chest, and into his arm. A fiery bolt formed in his fingers.

Yuri separated her arms in a rapid movement. The sphere took flight quickly and bounced off the walls. He cocked his arm back and slung his bolt through the air. It soared like lightning striking and collided with the sphere, which exploded with energy that looked like stardust. Its sizzling fragments fell to the ground like rain.

Grey Cloak let out a triumphant "Ha-ha!"

Yuri summoned her own bolts of green energy in her hands then flung them both at him.

He started to duck but spread his fingers out instead. A round shield of radiant blue energy formed in his palm. It caught the full force of the flying bolts. "Gah!" The magic fire burned with shocking effect. He flicked his wrist and summoned another one of his bolts and flung it back.

Yuri jumped and rolled underneath a table then popped up behind a shield of her own and flung more bolts like a wild woman. Shards of lightning zinged back and forth. They exploded into walls and whistled overhead.

Grey Cloak's shield faded and died after a blinding collision with Yuri's bolt. His arms shook again. Yuri closed in on him with her hands full of fire. He had one bolt left in hand and hurled it at the chandelier. Its chain snapped, and it fell on Yuri with a loud crash.

"Yuri!"

He rushed to her aid and lifted the chandelier from her body. She was lying on the ground, not moving. He rolled her over onto her back, and her eyes snapped open. She jabbed him in the chest with fingers filled with shocking energy.

Grey Cloak's hairs stood on end, his body swayed, and the day went black. The last thing he remembered was Yuri laughing.

28

CRACK SCOWL

Rhonna marched through the cold rain down the muddy road toward Crack Scowl with Lythlenion in tow. They made their way through the eastern gates that led into the large city.

Crack Scowl was a dreary city. Its tall buildings were made from blocks of limestone and graying wood that appeared rickety. The wind howled through the smoking chimneys, and the muddy roads were half paved. The citizens pushed their way through the cold to their next destinations.

"Pardon you," Rhonna said to a man who had walked right over her toes.

The beefy man peered down at her with tired eyes and said, "Stuff it, dwarf!"

As the man moved on, she stuck her foot out and

caught his toe. He stumbled into another man, who was bigger than he was.

"Watch where you're going!" the larger man said.

The beefy citizen pushed up his sleeves and said, "Do you want to make something of it, fat face?"

Rhonna didn't stick around to see what happened, but she did hear the distinct sound of a fist smacking into a face. She gave a razor-thin smile.

"I see that," Lythlenion said. He had his traveler's cloak drawn around his body, and a hood was covering his head. "I thought we were maintaining a low profile."

"Eh." She didn't care at all for Crack Scowl. The people were as miserable as the weather. "They'll live."

The city was busy, crammed with thousands of people shoving their way through the streets. Carts and wagons were pulled by mules and horses. People shouted at the tops of their lungs at one another as they tried to squeeze past. Fights and scuffles broke out. Pockets were picked, and vagrants fled through the streets.

Soldiers patrolled the streets en masse. At least two could be seen on every corner. They carried wooden clubs and wore sword belts and daggers with leather armor. Scale-mail coifs covered their heads, giving them a menacing and formidable look. Not one of them was slight in build, either. They were brutes, mostly orcs and men, quick to strike and bludgeon anyone who didn't follow their commands.

Rhonna averted her eyes from the soldiers when she snaked by. She knifed her way between a moving pair of horse-drawn wagons and squeezed into the back streets, which weren't as crowded, and aimed for a weathered two-story stone building at the end of the road. Its shutters were battened down. Smoke streamed out of the chimney. A single door led inside. An old man with a full beard was standing with his back to the wall, under the eaves, smoking a pipe. A wooden sign that read Rooty's Rest was mounted over the door.

Lythlenion pushed the door open. "Ladies first."

She shoved him in the back. "Get in there."

A young halfling man with curly blond hair greeted them. "Welcome to—"

Rhonna and Lythlenion took their cloaks off and threw them at the halfling, covering him with them.

He flailed under the soaking-wet garments and said, "Rooty's!"

The tavern floor was caked in mud. Men and women were huddled over their candlelit tables, talking. It smelled like baked bread and greasy food. Lythlenion's stomach grumbled. Rhonna spied Zora and Tanlin sitting in the back of the tavern beside a small fireplace that had stuffed chickens standing on the mantle.

Tanlin stood and bowed. He had grown a short gray beard, and his clothing was well-made. "Well met, friends."

Rhonna pulled up a chair and sat down. Lythlenion did the same.

"It's good to see you both well," Lythlenion said.

"You too." Zora squeezed Lythlenion's hand. "Hungry?"

"Famished."

Tanlin eased back into his chair and flagged a barmaid down. "I'm pretty good with reading faces. I take it that you haven't had any fortune finding Dyphestive either?"

Rhonna rubbed her face. "Dark Mountain is buttoned up like a quarry gnome in his hole. The only thing we've been doing is watching the Long Road. Nothing. No Dyphestive. No Doom Riders. The same as last month. You?"

"I still have feelers out between Black Stow and Far Stick. Zora and I have been to both cities twice in the last month," Tanlin said. "Not many people in Ugrad will speak about Black Frost and his minions. Still, we keep inquiring."

The barmaid brought over a tray of steaming food and tankards of ale and put them on the table.

Lythlenion dragged a plate of meat and boiled red potatoes over and said, "My thanks."

Rhonna drank all the ale in her tankard before the barmaid could step away and said, "Two more." She pulled out a cigar and lit it with the candle centered on the table then puffed it a few times and blew a big smoke ring. "This isn't getting it done."

"Where's Bowbreaker?" Zora asked.

"He doesn't want to take his eyes off of the Long Road. You know him," Rhonna said. "Hates cities too."

Zora gave a disappointed look. "Perhaps Tanlin and I should visit the Long Road. It's time that we switched things up."

Rhonna arched an eyebrow. "No, we stick with it. If no one has seen the Doom Riders, then they must still be in Dark Mountain."

"That doesn't mean that Dyphestive is with them. If anything, he'll be back with the Riskers. Or in Dark Mountain's prisons," Tanlin said.

"No, but they will know where he is, won't they?" she said.

Tanlin looked appalled. "You aren't seriously suggesting that we rattle a Doom Rider? Do I need to remind you that they killed our friends?"

Rhonna eyed the man and said, "I know what they did, but what choice do we have?"

29

"I don't mean to insult you, Rhonna, but you are mad," Zora said with her fists balled up on the table. "The Doom Riders are a pack, are they not?"

"Possibly. We don't know that for sure. If one comes out of the black crests, then we'll take him or her down." Rhonna picked up a fork and a knife and started sawing into the roasted beef. "That's my plan."

"That's a horrible plan. You'll bring doom down on all of us, and what good would that do Dyphestive?" Tanlin shook his head. "Listen, we are as impatient as you are, but we've been discussing another idea. A simpler and safer idea."

Lythlenion washed down his food and said, "I'd like to hear it." He slid his gaze toward Rhonna. "What do you say?"

She kept her eyes down and said, "I'm listening."

Zora's tight expression eased. "Good. Well, over the past few months, Tanlin and I have built a few relationships with other merchants. After all, we are clothing merchants. Those merchants have connections with the powers that be at Dark Mountain. I could enter with those merchants, posing as a servant girl."

"A spy? If they discover you, they'll kill you," Rhonna said. "It's too risky, not to mention they'll use you to find us out."

"This is what I do, Rhonna."

Eyeing Tanlin, Rhonna asked, "How do you know that you can trust these merchants?"

He clasped his fingers together and said, "As I've mentioned before, I am a member of the Brotherhood of Whispers. We are all united in the same cause—keeping the peace on Gapoli. Black Frost is a threat to that. He has many enemies, seen and unseen."

Rhonna licked her teeth. She was a patient woman and wasn't one to rush anything, but she knew that the longer she let time pass, the more likely she would lose Dyphestive. She couldn't let that happen. The time for waiting was over. It was time to act. "I can't believe I'm saying this, but—"

Zora slapped her hands on the table. "Yes!" She stood up and moved around the table.

"Don't you dare hug me." Rhonna cringed.

"Fine." Zora gave Lythlenion a big hug.

Lythlenion patted her arms and grinned.

"I'm going to get prepared immediately. Come on, Tanlin."

He nodded but had a worried look in his eyes. As Zora hurried up the stairs, he passed by Rhonna and said, "I wasn't prepared for you to say yes."

"Me, either."

Lythlenion watched Tanlin disappear up the stairs. He started back into his meal and said, "I wasn't prepared, either. That's a leap of faith for you."

"I know. I like the girl, and I don't want to see her hurt, but we can't wait forever. It's time to find out what happened to Dyphestive. Whether he's alive or not."

"Perhaps you've feared that he might be dead. That is why you don't want to find out."

"Of course I fear that. Even I can admit it." She tilted her tankard up to her lips and drained the ale halfway down. "I wish we could get in there and find out for ourselves."

"They say that Dark Mountain is the same as any other city, only built into the rocks and stones. It's not very much different from many others. It's only run by monarchs that worship Black Frost. I wouldn't mind seeing it for myself. I've heard that streets are paved in silver and gold. Gemstones glint from the lampposts."

"Ha. That, I would like to see. How could such a dark place be filled with beauty?"

"That's by design. Evil covers itself in beauty to hide the darkness that lurks within."

"And you want to see it?"

He shrugged. "I can't help but be curious." He propped his war mace against the side of the mantel then reached over and took Rhonna's hammer from her lap and set it aside as well. "Let's enjoy this meal, shall we?"

"*Enjoy* is a stretch. I've chewed grass that tastes better."

"You've chewed grass?"

"It's a dwarven statement not meant to be taken literally but to be insulting."

Lythlenion chuckled. "I know. I was only teasing you. Have you ever relaxed?"

Rhonna chewed her food, swallowed, and said, "No, and I don't plan on it anytime soon, either."

The tavern door opened and brought a chill wind with it.

"Shut the door, you fool!" a tavern dweller hollered out.

Rhonna and Lythlenion turned in their chairs. A figure wrapped in soaking-wet robes was standing in the doorway. Her long hair covered her face. The dripping wet woman walked past the halfling greeter and stood in front of the fireplace. With her head down, she warmed her long, slender fingers in front of the fire and asked in a quiet voice, "Where is Tanlin?"

30

DARK MOUNTAIN

The sun had come up over the mountains like a giant burning eye. The rocky black hilltops twinkled with frost. Dragons darted over the skyline. Dyphestive's face slammed into the dirt.

Scar chortled. "Bruh-huh-huh! What's the matter, boy? Can't you catch a ghost?"

Dyphestive's cheek was pinned in the dirt, his arm was twisted behind him, and Ghost's knee was jammed in his back. Pain raced through his joints and ligaments, and the ever-silent Brother of Destruction bent his arm behind his head. He groaned and wiggled to pull free. "Urrrgh!"

Ghost twisted Dyphestive's arm harder and bent his wrist back.

Legs flailing, Dyphestive tapped out. "Yield! Yield!"

"Look at that—he quit already," Scar said. "He's nothing but a boy."

Dyphestive rolled onto his broad back as soon as Ghost let go and stood up. After he'd caught his breath, he sat back up. He rolled his shoulders and rubbed his wrists. Ghost hadn't broken anything, but it sure felt like it. He was throbbing from head to toe.

"I'd have broken his wrist and his arm and his neck," Scar said, his breath visible in the cold. He was sitting on a stone wall that surrounded their barracks. It was a bleak environment, private, and surrounded by the gloomy mountain range that was iced over in the bitter cold. "Is it my turn?"

All of the Doom Riders were present, including Drysis. All of them were wearing the dragon-scale armor.

Drysis's spiked white hair had grown out, and she'd put it in a braid that ran over her shoulders. She still had the eye patch covering her left eye, and the other eye was rimmed with kohl. Casually leaning against the wall, she was twirling a crossbow bolt between her fingers. "You can have your turn, Scar. But first, give Dyphestive some water. He looks thirsty."

"Water? Huh!" Scar slung a waterskin at Dyphestive.

He caught the skin, tore the top off, and drank. Every day for months, they'd come outside to the courtyard and fought. That day, it was wrestling. The next, it would be weapons. All of it with backbreaking chores in between. He hated all of it, but he hung in there. He never wanted to go back in the pit again. He could feel the bugs crawling all over him when he thought about it. It made him shiver.

"He's one thirsty lad," Shamrok said. "I can't drink my ale that fast to save my life. Say, Drysis, how much of this worthless lingering are we going to do? Shouldn't we be doing more important things than training this mule?"

"We go when Black Frost gives me orders and when he's ready," she said.

"He'll never be ready at this rate. He's strong but can't fight. We've taught him all that we know." Shamrok gave Dyphestive a pitying look. "Not enough wicked in him."

"Agreed! I've been saying it since we started. He's a mule, like Shamrok says. Only good for moving heavy things." Scar spit on the ground. "He'll be no use to us in a fight."

Dyphestive stood and tossed the waterskin on the ground. "I can whip you."

Scar sneered. "Now that's what I like to hear." He slid his big frame off the wall and approached. "Step aside, Ghost. I'll break what you didn't."

Ghost stood in Scar's path and wagged a finger in the bigger man's face.

"Oh, you want to go with me?" Scar grinned. "Anytime, silent one."

Dyphestive clenched his fingers then released them. *I would love to see Ghost tear him apart, but I would rather do it myself.* He hadn't been as much of a dullard as they'd made him out to be. The Brothers of Destruction might be training him, but he was learning more about them as well. Ghost was the fastest and best at hand-to-hand and wrestling. Scar was the natural brawler of the three. He would take up a heavy sword or axe first and swing it with raw power. Shamrok was in the middle—well-balanced, quick on his feet for a large man, more patient, and calculating. He was the easiest to fight of the three. He didn't make Dyphestive feel like he was going to kill him every time, but Shamrok still brought the pain. Drysis was the only one that he hadn't fought. She was a mystery, but her men were loyal hounds who would lick her boots if she told them to, even though they smarted off from time to time.

"Step aside, Ghost," she said. "The two of you can play later. I want to see how the big boy handles himself with Scar today."

Ghost moved over to the wall then hopped on it and squatted like a frog.

Dyphestive and Scar circled. Even though Dyphestive had grown, Scar was still a noticeably bigger man and looked like a juggernaut in his armor. Dyphestive hated Scar. The man had tormented him from day one. He wanted to kill him.

Scar gyrated his arms and flexed his fingers at the same

time. "Make the first move, boy. Let's see what you've learned."

Dyphestive wiped his forearm across his mouth. He'd learned plenty: headlocks, hammer locks, quarter knots, choke holds, leg sweeps, hip tosses, and numerous takedowns. The only problem was that he wasn't better than they were—but that day, that was going to change. He charged Scar hard and fast.

They locked their hands behind each other's necks and bumped foreheads. Then they twisted and tossed from side to side, trying to throw each other.

Scar's boots slid backward across the ground, but he dug his toes in and pushed back. "Come on, boy! I know you want to take me! You hate me! Show it to me!"

Dyphestive dropped to a knee and pulled Scar down on his shoulder then flipped the man onto the ground.

Shamrok let out a wild cry. "That's it, Dyphestive! Teach him a lesson. Bust his face in!"

He had Scar locked up from behind. It was the first time he'd ever gotten an advantage on the man. He picked Scar up by the waist and slammed him hard into the ground.

Scar let out a loud "Argh! You runt!" Then he turned his legs under his hips and wrenched his body out of Dyphestive's mighty grip. He pointed a finger at him. "You'll pay for that."

"We'll see." Confidence flowed through Dyphestive's

body. It was the first time he'd taken any of them down. He saw growing concern in Scar's ugly face.

They locked together again. Scar shoved Dyphestive to the ground with his side. He hit on the side of his face and tried to scramble up, but Scar snatched Dyphestive's hand and twisted it backward. He ground his teeth and fought against the blinding pain.

"I bet that hurts, boy! Yield!"

Dyphestive was on his knees with his limbs trembling. His shoulder burned like fire, and his wrist felt like it was about to break.

"Give in, boy. Quit! Quit again like you always do!"

Wrestling had rules. One of them was no punching. Dyphestive broke that rule and walloped Scar in the gut. Another rule was no headbutting, but he lunged and busted Scar's wide nose on his forehead.

Scar staggered back, his face contorted with rage. "Now you're going to die!"

31

The fight turned ugly quickly. Dyphestive stood his ground as he and Scar whaled on each other with hammer-like blows. There wasn't any skill to any of it. It was two warriors standing toe-to-toe, trying to kill each other.

A hard shot in the jaw wobbled Dyphestive's knees. He threw an uppercut that glanced off of Scar's lantern-shaped jaw. Back and forth, they went. *Whop! Crack! Boom!* They exchanged a flurry of punches to the face and down the body. Murder was in both of their eyes.

Scar locked Dyphestive's arm and started delivering hard shots to the ribs. He groaned and went down.

"Getting tired, boy?" Scar went to work on the ribs, hitting them harder and harder, gaining strength as he did so. "You look tired. What's the matter? Can't you hit back?"

His head hung down to his chest. He didn't have much left. The Doom Riders had been working him every day to exhaustion. All he had was the fire churning inside him—the deep, growing hatred of Scar. He rammed his forearm at Scar's crotch with all of his remaining strength.

"Oooh, right in the nanoos!" Shamrok hollered. "Boy, I've never seen Scar's eyes so big before. I swear I felt that one myself!"

Scar was doubled over with his face reddening. "You're going to pay for that." He caught Dyphestive in a headlock and squeezed with all of his might. "Good riddance, mule!"

He clawed at Scar's arms and fought to stand, but Scar held him down. He was suffocating.

"Enough, Scar!" Drysis said.

The wicked man didn't relent.

"I said enough!"

After a bright flash of light came instant pain, like a thousand needles poking the insides of Dyphestive's body. Scar fell away and landed on his hands and knees. Dyphestive fell flat on his side, twitching. As he strained to lift his head, wisps of white energy danced on Drysis's fingertips. They faded away, leaving her smoldering good eye glaring at the both of them.

She walked over to Scar and kicked him hard in the ribs. "You try my patience. Keep it up, and I'll replace you with him."

"I would never betray you, Drysis," Scar said. He sat up

and pushed his nose into place with a disturbing *crunch.* "It's him that you should be worried about."

"I don't worry. Apparently, you do. That's weakness."

"What?" Scar stood up, and his hot stare landed on her. "You can call me a lot of things, but don't call me weak."

"You disagree." She moved and stood toe-to-toe with the man and looked slightly down into his eyes. Out of nowhere, she picked Scar up and hoisted him over her head then threw him like a bale of hay into the wall.

Scar's body burst through the rocks, and he sank to the ground, clutching his side, eyes wide.

She stared him down. "Like I said. Weak."

Dyphestive stared at the towering woman. *How did she do that?*

He watched her flex her fingers and studied the chain mail that ran the length of her left arm. She was muscular for a woman but not nearly as brawny as the men that she was surrounded by.

Drysis caught him looking at her. "Is there something that you would like to say?"

"I didn't think a woman could be so strong, let alone a man. You must be really angry inside."

"I'm not angry. I'm hungry. Shamrok, Ghost, finish out his day with double the labor on the mountain. Scar, get your sorry tail up and come with me." She turned and walked away toward the barracks.

Scar was holding his arm when he walked away and

had murder in his eyes when he looked at Dyphestive. He stopped in front of Shamrok, who grabbed his arm and popped the dislocated shoulder back into place.

Scar didn't bat an eye. He pointed at Dyphestive. "You're mine." Then he hurried after Drysis.

Shamrok held a hand out and helped Dyphestive to his feet. "I have to hand it to you—you're one tough nugget. Scar hits harder than the rest of us, and you're still breathing." He poked Dyphestive's sore ribs with his fingers. "None of them is broken, and you don't have any armor on. Heh." He glanced at Ghost. "Must have bones harder than iron, like I said." He flicked Dyphestive in the head. "And a thick skull to match it. Come on. Long day ahead. Grab the wheelbarrow. It's time to climb the hill of death again."

32

___

CRACK SCOWL

K *nock. Knock. Knock.*

Zora and Tanlin were upstairs in their tavern room, making preparations, when soft knocking came at the door.

She opened the door and found Lythlenion's pleasant face staring at her. "Is something wrong?"

"No, I don't think so. A woman is downstairs, elven, very beautiful. She asked for you and Tanlin," Lythlenion said.

Zora found Tanlin's eyes and gave him a curious look. He was folding up a shirt and stuffing it in a pack. He had an eyebrow arched.

"What more can you tell us about this woman?" Tanlin asked.

Lythlenion rubbed the white hairs on his chin and said,

"Well, she's stunning, tall, and well tanned for an elf. She's sort of mysterious."

"Tatiana!" Zora pushed by Lythlenion and left him gaping in the hallway. She raced down the hall and halfway down the stairs and peered into the tavern.

Tatiana was sitting at a table, talking with Rhonna. She locked eyes with Zora immediately. Zora jumped over the railing, startled a barmaid, and crossed the room in three giant bounds.

Tatiana stood up just in time to catch Zora with open arms. She gave her a warm and strong embrace.

"Lords of the Air, I've missed you!" Zora said, squeezing her tightly.

"I've missed you too. Very much." Tatiana kissed the top of Zora's head and rubbed her back. "How have you been?"

Zora broke the embrace and took a longer look at the eye-catching woman. She'd always thought that Tatiana was absolutely beautiful. The elven woman's gorgeous locks of dark hair were bound up and braided. It showed off more of the perfect features of her teardrop-shaped elven face. Her beautiful eyes were curious and probing, like a cat's. Zora placed her hands on her hips and said, "Well, it hasn't been the best of times, but it's better that you are here. I take it that you and Rhonna have become acquainted?"

"Very well," Tatiana said.

"Good, we women need to stick together." She chuckled and pulled up a chair.

Rhonna guzzled down another tankard of ale and burped. Then she hammered the table with her fist. "Another!"

Tatiana lifted her eyebrows.

"You'll get used to it," Zora said. She combed her hair behind her ear. "Um, are you going to be here long? How did you find us? I'm so sorry about Dalsay. I should have asked—I mean, we never got to... Well, you know, you had to go." She locked her hands on Tatiana's wrists. Her eyes were wet with tears. All of the memories of Adanadel, Dalsay, and Browning came flooding back. "I'm so glad you are here."

"Everything is fine, little sister. I'm glad that I'm here too. I've been looking for a long time and finally caught up with you. It hasn't been easy, but being a sorceress, I have special help." Tatiana patted her friend's hand. "As for me, I am doing well. I've spent most of my time at the Wizard Watch, preparing myself, now that Dalsay is gone."

"Preparing yourself for what?" Zora asked.

"To be the new leader of Talon."

Rhonna stopped drinking and set her tankard down. "Beg pardon?"

"With Adanadel and Dalsay gone, Talon will need a new leader. I've been preparing for months to fill their shoes. The quest for the dragon charms continues. That is why I sought you out, to start the group anew."

Rhonna's jaw clenched, and Zora's heart thumped. She'd become comfortable with Rhonna leading and wasn't at all comfortable with Tatiana stepping in. She loved the woman like a sister but had never figured her for a strong leader.

"Is there a problem?" Tatiana asked. Her stare moved between Zora and Rhonna.

Zora's chest tightened. Rhonna's face looked like it was about to burst.

At that moment, Tanlin and Lythlenion came down the stairs. Tanlin had a smile on his face as broad as a river.

He took Tatiana's hand and kissed it. "Tatiana, what an overwhelming surprise!"

"It's a surprise, all right," Rhonna grumbled.

The men took a seat at the table.

"How in the world did you find us?" Tanlin continued.

"I have my resources," Tatiana said. "I'm glad you are here, Tanlin, and it warms my heart to know that you are all well. I was worried."

"As were we," Tanlin said politely.

"I'm glad that you are here now. Are there any others?"

"Bowbreaker," Lythlenion said.

Rhonna shot him a fiery look.

"What? Did I say something wrong?"

"No, but the elven princess did. It seems that she has

plans to take charge of the company," Rhonna said. "And we've settled that."

"What do mean? What is this about?" Tanlin asked.

"I've been instructed by the Wizard Watch to take over Dalsay and Adanadel's purpose. The quest to retrieve the dragon charms must continue. I'm to lead those expeditions, the same as they did."

Zora caught Tanlin's eye. His face showed the same concerns about Tatiana that she had. In the meantime, Rhonna looked like she might explode as her face started to turn red.

"Listen, elfy," Rhonna said. "You might not be aware of this, but we have our own thing going on. We won't be backing away from it anytime soon, either."

"Is that so?"

Rhonna leaned over the table and poked it with her finger as she said, "That is so."

Tatiana leaned back in her chair and crossed her arms over her chest. "Tanlin, what is this all about?"

"We are still searching for Dyphestive. Our plans to rescue him have not changed. We are still trying to locate him now," Tanlin said.

"I see, but the dragon charms must take priority. I need you. I need all of you now." She looked down her nose at Rhonna. "We are still members of Talon, and there is a hierarchy. I'm at the top of that post. As for Rhonna and Lythlenion, they are not officially a part of the group. Just because we lost our friends doesn't mean that Talon disbanded. So far as the Wizard Watch is concerned, it's still in full effect."

Rhonna scooted her chair back so fast that she knocked it over when she stood up. "That's fine by me, lady. You can call all of the shots you want, but Lythlenion and I won't be here to listen. Come on, Lyth. We're going."

33

"Did I say something wrong?" Tatiana asked.

"You might have come over a little strong," Zora commented. It seemed like Tatiana was trying to act like Dalsay, and if she was, it had come across extremely awkwardly. Dalsay was straightforward, but it came naturally with him. With Tatiana, one wouldn't expect that sort of inner toughness. "Rhonna's not thin-skinned by any means, but we've had leadership issues already."

"Ah, and she's been leading?"

"More or less. She's not so bad at it," Tanlin said.

Tatiana frowned, and her chin dipped into her chest. "I see. I tried to tell the Wizard Watch that I wasn't suited for this. But they didn't give me a choice. I told them that I'm not like Dalsay or Adanadel, but they insisted." She sighed. "I'm sorry."

That was the softer side of Tatiana, the side that Zora was used to. She could relate better to that. She petted her friend's arm. "I'm no leader, either, but that doesn't mean you aren't." She didn't know what else to say.

"Tatiana, you are a strong woman. We know this. But you have to be who you are. Don't try to be like Dalsay or Adanadel. And they weren't perfect leaders, by any means, were they? But they had the final say. You've been given this charge. Be yourself," Tanlin said.

"That makes sense," she said. She sniffed and wiped her nose. "The Wizard Watch never told me anything. They only say do. So you do. I'm sorry I offended your friends."

"They are tough. Trust me, they'll get over it," Zora said. "Don't you remember all of the arguments that you had with Dalsay? Remember that time he wanted to cross Midburn Bridge and fight the swamp walkers that guarded it?"

"Yes, he was in a hurry," Tatiana said.

"Who talked him out of it and found a better way?"

"I did."

"That is the person that we need," Tanlin said. "And just so you know, Rhonna isn't half bad. Perhaps you can work together, to start."

Tatiana nodded. "Perhaps." She took a deep breath. "You know, mastering the intricacies of spell casting is much easier to master than relationships with people. People are unpredictable."

"Agreed," Zora said. She leaned over the table. "Tell us about the mission."

"There is a dragon charm near the hills of Far Stick. There, we must go. Or I must go."

Tanlin rested his arm on the table and said, "Tatiana, are you aware of what we are trying to achieve here?"

"I have some knowledge. I know that you want to locate Dyphestive, and the Wizard Watch told me that Grey Cloak is alive and with the Sky Riders."

"Yes, and we are hoping to find Dyphestive before we rendezvous with Grey Cloak and Anya after one year. We'd come up with a new plan to try tonight, and coincidentally, you arrived."

"Wizards arrive when least expected." She tapped her fingers together and said, "Well, tell me your plans."

Zora filled her in on their plans to let her infiltrate Dark Mountain as a servant girl and hopefully locate Dyphestive.

"I almost feel guilty for admitting this, but I like it," Tatiana said. "It's selfish of me to say so, but while you are occupied with doing that, we can search out the dragon charm at Far Stick."

Tanlin drummed his fingers on the table and said, "Now all we have to do is convince Rhonna, assuming that we need muscle, like with our other adventures."

"If she disagrees, I have some help that I brought with me," Tatiana said.

"Henchmen?" Zora raised an eyebrow. "They don't work out so well."

"No, they are more than that."

"Where are they?" Tanlin asked.

"Outside."

"In the rain?"

"I didn't want them to disturb anyone. They're... well, different."

Tanlin scratched the back of his head.

Zora shrugged and asked, "Shall we meet them?"

Tatiana nodded. "The sooner, the better, I guess." She led the way out of the tavern.

Zora and Tanlin grabbed their cloaks on the way out and stepped off the porch stoop into the chilly rain. When they met up with Tatiana, she was standing in the middle of the narrow road.

"Your friends are out here?" Zora asked. She didn't see anyone down the road.

Tanlin tapped on her shoulder.

She turned toward the tavern. "Yes?" Then she froze.

Two figures were squatting beside the tavern's entrance and started to stand up.

Zora's gaze moved upward as the person on the right grew taller and taller. Her jaw dropped. His shoulders were huge, and he had horns on his head. He was a Minotaur. "Oh my."

"Why, thank you," the person on the other side of the

Minotaur said. He was a handsome, fit man with short hair and blackened leather armor. He had two swords crossed over his back and short swords on his hips, complemented by daggers along with two bandoliers of knives criss-crossing his chest. He also had daggers sheathed around his thighs and his boots. "It's not as astonished as I expected, but I'll take it."

Zora had never seen a man wearing so many weapons before. It would have been completely ridiculous, but every weapon the man was carrying was crafted to his body perfectly. As for the Minotaur, well, he was huge, over seven feet of brawn, horns, and muscle. His face was that of a bison, with the curled horns of a ram. He had hooved feet that had sunk in the mud.

Tatiana moved alongside the men, but before she could speak, the swordsman stepped forward. "I'm Reginald, but my foes know me as Razor." He whisked the swords from their scabbards in the wink of an eye, spun them around his wrists, and sheathed them. "The greatest blade master in the world."

"Impressive," Zora said. She noticed Tatiana giving a slight eye roll.

Reginald the Razor strolled over to the Minotaur and said in a charming voice, "This is Grunt. He's not one for talking—you know their tongues are so big." He held his hand under Grunt's jaw and opened his mouth then elbowed the Minotaur, who was barely covered in his oversized cloak. "Grunt, show them your tongue. It's bigger than my head."

"That's quite all right. I'll take your word for it," Zora said.

"Anyway," Razor continued, "Grunt grunts when he speaks, and I interpret. As you can see, he's a mountain of muscle, likes to kill and smash things, and enjoys every food imaginable. He can even eat grass, too, in case we are low on rations."

Grunt grunted.

"I was only teasing." Razor eyed the brute. "Try to have a sense of humor, will you." He held his hand to the side of his mouth and whispered, "I'm not kidding. He really does eat grass and straw and is embarrassed about it. A real sore spot." He strolled over to Zora. "And what is your name, dearie?"

"I'm Zora, and this is Tanlin," she said. Razor didn't have a crack in his skin, but his strong hands were calloused. She guessed him to be little older than her, possibly twenty. As for the Minotaur, she had no idea, nor had she seen one before. Minotaurs were very reclusive and lived far south in Sultur Slay.

Razor kissed her hand. "Splendid to meet the both of you, especially you, Zora." He winked. "You are a light in the darkness. A rose among the thatches. A cool breeze that kisses the hot sun from your face. A—"

"I think she gets the picture, Reginald," Tatiana said. "And I thought *I* was the light in the darkness."

He snickered. "As my father always says, two candles are better than one."

"You'll have to forgive him. He's very chatty," Tatiana said. She pulled her cloak around her body. "Let's go find your friends Rhonna and Lythlenion. Lead the way."

"Rhonna," Razor uttered with curiosity. "I like the sound of that."

Zora and Tanlin shared glances and hid their giggles.

HIDEMARK

Day in and day out, Grey Cloak worked. He trained, he cooked, he trained, he slept, then he woke and trained more. His mind was about to burst from new knowledge as they taught him the same routines and information over and over again. But he couldn't have cared less. He liked the Sky Riders, but the truth was, he wanted out. And the first break he got, he went for it.

His hands found purchase on the sheer crater wall that encircled the area called Hidemark. The rocky walls were covered in vines and loose vegetation. Hand over hand, with his bare toes digging for footing, he climbed like a monkey. *Almost there.*

The rim of the crater was over one thousand feet up. It was the wee hours of the morning, and he'd stolen away from Hidemark's chambers. Normally, one of the Sky

Riders watched over the entrance that led inside Hidemark, but that night it was Hammerjaw, who was a notorious sleeper and snorer. Grey Cloak had taken his cloak, slipped by the sleepy dwarf, and stolen away into the woods. Come first light, he would be long gone. *Catch me if you can.*

By the time he reached the top of the crater, his arms and shoulders were burning. The climb had taken a lot more out of him than he'd figured. Still, he managed to lift his arms in triumph and look down into the dark jungle from whence he'd just escaped. He breathed in the fresh air.

The sky is all yours, Sky Riders.

He cast his stare outward toward Lake Flugen. It stretched on for leagues, but he could make out the far-distant beaches. All he needed to do was find or built a watercraft of some kind. Perhaps he could swim it and escape. He searched Lake Gunderland's beaches. The sand twinkled from the moonlight, and he ran his gaze along the coast. *No giants that I can see. I wonder where they sleep. Oh well, no time to find out.*

The outer rim of the dormant volcano wasn't as sheer as it was within. He could navigate the rugged junglelike forest by running. The paleness of his bare feet was hidden by the rich-green foliage. His cloak didn't snag on a single branch as he ran. Once he hit the bottom, he realized that he'd been swallowed up by the lush terrain of great trees and vines that were thicker than his legs. *I didn't foresee this.*

Grey Cloak could no longer see the beach, which must have been a league above him. The huge leaves blocked his view of the sky. He'd been swallowed up in jungle blackness.

He cupped his ear. Bugs chirped. Critters jumped through the tree branches. His nose twitched. He could smell water and hear the wind. Taking his best guess, he started onward, pushed through ferns that were taller than he was, and ducked through the low-hanging branches. He walked for what must have been an hour and found no sign of the shore.

He was lost. *No wonder they dropped me on the mess of an island. There's no way out of it! Zooks!*

35

*D*on't panic. *Day will come, and you'll be able to see your way out.*

A snake as thick as tree roots slithered over his toes. Grey Cloak froze. *Nice snake.* It vanished underneath the heavy brush.

Something moved in the treetops, and Grey Cloak lifted his eyes. Some sort of monkey was moving from tree to tree. *Why didn't I think of that?*

He climbed the tree all the way to the top, about thirty feet high, and pushed his way through the highest leaves. He sat among a bed of treetops that went on in all directions. The mountainous crater that he'd crawled from was behind him, and the lake's beaches were only a few hundred yards away.

"Ha! I'm practically on top of it. I knew it. Never doubted for a moment."

Grey Cloak climbed down the tree, got his bearings, and ran in a straight line for the beach, not stopping until his toes hit the soft white sand. He scooped the sand up in his hands and flung it all over. "Yes!"

He quieted his voice and looked about, not wanting to alert any giants, or anything else troublesome, for that matter.

With the lakeshore breeze blowing, he stepped out to the water's edge. Small, choppy waves broke along the shoreline. The other side was far, far away. By the stars and the moon, he could tell that he was facing north. He hitched his pants up and waded knee deep into the water. *Not bad. The question is, can I swim it, or do I need a boat?*

Plenty of trees were around to craft a small boat. He could bind it with rope from Hidemark. The Sky Riders had taught him many practical crafts and skills over the last few months, and he could put it to work to serve his ambitions. But there was another issue—the water giants.

Anya had told him that giants who lived in the lake waters destroyed any craft that tried to invade Gunder Island's beaches. If that was the case, he would have to find another way.

But she might have been lying to me to keep me on the island. She doesn't seem like a liar, though. Perhaps she stretches the truth. Most good liars do.

A sucking sound deep in the wet sand caught his ear. When he looked down, holes the size of his fist were popping up around his feet, water bubbling out of them. *What in Gapoli is that?*

He squatted, and the holes began to expand. A crab claw popped out of the sand. It was as big as his arm, hard, and so jacked that it could snap a man in twain.

The claw snapped at Grey Cloak's leg, and he jumped away like a jackrabbit. More giant crabs burst out from underneath the sand. Each and every one was almost as big as he was. Two deep, dozens of crabs circled him. Their front pincers snapped open and closed as they moved in.

"Zooks!" Grey Cloak danced away from a pair of pincers that would have cut his leg in half. Another crab closed in, and he jumped away only to dodge another and another. The crabs pushed him to his limits as they scurried across the sand. Their tiny eyes stood up from small antenna on their heads, probing him.

Grey Cloak danced for his life, and the crabs came closer and closer. The tips of their pincers nipped at his cloak. One wrong move, and they would have him. *This isn't working!*

Four crabs that had surrounded him closed in as one. He jumped over one set of pincers and landed on another crab's back. *Snap! Clack! Snap!*

The crabs came at him, crawling over one another like hungry juggernauts. He ran over their porcelain-colored bodies, like a frog hopping from lily pad to lily pad. He would jump on one shell, and another crab would attack. He tried to angle away from the moving knot of crustaceans, but wherever he went, they went. *This is madness!*

His feet touched sand, and it sank beneath him. Another crab emerged below him, and he rose on its back. He jumped, rolled, slid through closing pincers, and spun away from their lethal claws. *I can't keep this up forever!*

With his lungs burning, Grey Cloak searched for an avenue to escape. There was league of beaches all around him, but the crabs were so thick that he couldn't get past them. If he could only get beyond their ranks, he could sprint away. *They'll never catch me then.*

As he hopped and danced away from death, he suddenly regretted his decision to leave. He would be more than happy to be back in his alcove and going to bed. Clearly, Gunder Island and its surrounding waters were too dangerous. His doubt stirred him, however. It made him angry. *This is all their fault, anyway. I won't let the Sky Riders win. I don't need them. I'll show them!*

His keen eyes picked up a path in the crabs' ranks where their claws were lowered, one right behind the other, five crabs deep. Grey Cloak didn't hesitate. He launched himself on top of the nearest crab with its pincers lowered. Its pincers stretched back and snapped.

He leaped to the next crab. The moment his toes touched, its pincers rose, but he'd already leapt to the next one. It happened three more times, then he was free of the crustacean mob. He ran, and the crabs chased him.

Sand flying from under his feet, he quickly distanced himself from the crabs. He turned around, ran backward, pointed, and laughed. "Ha-ha-ha! Stupid crabs, see if you can catch me now! Ha-haaa!"

Grey Cloak tumbled into a sinkhole—a deep one, but he managed to land on his feet. When he looked up, he realized it would be a climb to get up. He began it, but the sand broke away from the wall. The harder he dug, the more the wall collapsed.

"Oh no!" He clawed at the sinkhole wall desperately.

The crabs gathered around the edge and started pouring into the hole.

Grey Cloak hollered at the top of his lungs, "Heeelp!"

36

The crabs scurried into the hole. Grey Cloak pulled his dagger and started poking at their hard shells, but his blade skipped off them.

Crunch!

"Aaah!" he shouted, thinking that a crab had pinched through his bones. "Mercy me, I'm dying."

Crunch!

The hungry crabs that had filled the pit momentarily froze.

Grey Cloak wasn't certain what had happened, but whatever *crunched* wasn't him. *A dragon. It's a dragon!* "Cinder!" he called.

A large hand reached into the hole and wrapped around Grey Cloak's body. The powerful fingers crushed him in a viselike grip. "Gaaah!" He was lifted effortlessly out of the hole.

A giant, at least twenty feet tall, held Grey Cloak like a doll. His face was huge, and he had short shaggy hair and a flattened nose. He was wearing sewn-together hides of wild beasts that came up to cover one of his shoulders. His arms had rocklike muscle that bulged underneath flab. His feet stomped the crabs. *Crunch! Crunch! Crunch!*

The dozens of crabs that survived the giant's onslaught scurried over the white sands and back into the lake. Over half a dozen were dead at the giant's feet.

With lazy eyes, the giant peered down at the crabs and said in a low and booming voice, "Dinner."

Grey Cloak fought to keep his breath. His ribs were being crushed, and he could feel his eyeballs bugging out. With his free hand, he used his dagger to poke into the meat of the giant's hand.

The giant held him up to his face, his bushy unibrow knitted. His breath was like rotting seaweed, and when he said, "Don't do that," he showed his crooked teeth. His grip eased.

Grey Cloak gasped. "Oh, thank goodness!"

"You make good bait," the giant said with a toothy grin. When he spoke, his voice was so deep that Grey Cloak's skin vibrated. The giant picked up a crab and bit the pincers off and started chewing the crustacean.

The sound of the crab's shell breaking in the giant's

mouth jarred Grey Cloak as he cringed. The crab's body popped and crunched. It made the loudest, most horrible sound. He tried to pry his body free, but the giant's mighty grip was like Cinder's. He watched in profound horror as the giant ate crab after crab.

Grey Cloak mustered up the courage to speak. "You know, they would taste a lot better if you added butter."

The giant eyed him. "What is budder?"

He started to laugh but fought it back and said, "No, not budder—butter."

"Budder?"

"No, butter."

"Tell me about budder," the giant said.

"Well, it's yellow and creamy, and it makes your food, eh, taste better."

"Hmm." The giant sawed his finger between his lower lip and his bullish chin. "Like gold?"

"No, it's softer, eh, like a..." He looked around but didn't see anything like butter. "Well, it's hard to explain, I guess. Um, are you going to eat me?"

"No, no, you are good bait. I'll use you for fishing, little man."

"I'm an elf, actually."

"Little man, you help me fish. And you find me budder. It taste good, right?"

"Very good. Uh..." He stretched out his hand. "My name is Grey Cloak. What is your name?"

The giant scratched his head. "My family calls me Tontor."

Grey Cloak only knew a little bit about giants. He'd heard that they could be cunning from his discussions with Hammerjaw and Hogrim. But this giant appeared to be younger and not very smart. "Tontor. I like that name. It's a strong name. I was wondering, Tontor, would it be possible for us to become friends?"

"What is a friend?"

Perfect! "A friend is someone that will help you out. Like if I help you catch crabs or fish. And you could help me by, well, taking me to the other side of the lake."

"Tontor can't go to the other side of the lake. Tontor likes it here."

Grey Cloak leaned on the giant's finger and made himself comfortable. "Well, that's a shame. I guess it's too deep for you to cross. I wouldn't want you to get hurt."

Tontor's eyebrow wiggled, and his puffy lips curled. "Not too deep. Tontor walk all the way across on the bottom. And he swim too. Tontor hold his breath a mighty time. Tontor sleep beneath the waves."

"Oh, come now, you aren't that tall. I mean, look at that lake. It's deep."

Tontor shook his head. "No!" He suddenly dropped Grey Cloak, who landed with wide-eyed surprise on his feet. Tontor marched to the edge of the water. "Tontor show you!"

Grey Cloak ran after the giant. Tontor was waist-deep in the water by the time Grey Cloak had wet his feet on the breaking waves again. He flagged the giant down with his arms over his head and shouted, "No! Wait, Tontor! Wait!"

Tontor stopped and twisted around at the waist. "Tontor show you. Water not deep. Tontor is tall. You watch." He spoke like a child trying to prove himself. "I walk under the waves. I nap among the shells." He turned his back.

"No, Tontor, listen, I believe you. I believe you."

The waves crashed against Tontor's broad chest. He sank deeper into the water as he walked step after step. Another wave passed over his head. Then he vanished.

Water splashed over Grey Cloak's knees. "Dirty acorns. He's gone. My one shot to get across the lake has vanished. There's no telling when he'll come back."

37

As Grey Cloak backed away from the seashore, he glanced side to side. *I hope those crabs don't come back.*

He made his way over to the sinkhole that he'd fallen in. A pincer that Tontor had ripped off was lying on the ground. He picked it up. The claw filled his arms like a lamb. *Well, if I get hungry, I can always eat this. It would probably be pretty good once I roasted it over the fire.*

The sound of waves splashing caught his ear, and he turned. Tontor was walking back toward the shore. He dropped the pincer and hurried over to the giant.

"I told you that I could walk on the bottom of the lake," the giant gloated. He balled up his fist and placed it over his chest. "Tontor tall."

Grey Cloak stood in front of the giant, tapping his foot

and shaking his head. "I don't know, Tontor. I mean, how am I supposed to know that? After all, I wasn't in the water with you. I'm sure that you made it pretty far, but honestly, can you make it all the way across without drowning?"

Tontor shook his head. "Of course Tontor can!" He beat his chest with a fist. "Watch me!"

"Hold on, my friend. You see, that's the problem. I can't watch you without going with you." He paced over the sand. "I wish I could believe you. I really do, but there isn't any way to prove that."

"Tontor carry you," the giant suggested.

Perfect! Grey Cloak played along with the giant, who was falling right into his hands. "What are you suggesting?"

"Tontor carry you." He scooped Grey Cloak up and hoisted him over his head then started walking into the water.

Being gripped in the giant's power terrified Grey Cloak. It would only be him, the giant, and the open water. Like a careless child, Tontor ventured deeper into the lake, seemingly oblivious to the danger he posed to Grey Cloak.

But Grey Cloak stuck to his plan. There would be no turning back. "Tontor, *are you sure* that you can make it all the way to the other side?"

"Tontor can do it. Tontor hold his breath a long time."

"If you say so," he replied with a tremble in his voice. His body was jolted as he sank deeper and deeper into the water. He had a bad feeling in the pit of his stomach as the giant's head vanished under the water. Grey Cloak was suspended above the rolling waves by the giant's hands in the form of a great seat. The sinking feeling in his stomach grew as his descent stopped.

"Huh," he said as he cast his gaze over the black water, which shimmered in the moonlight. Grey Cloak cold feel the giant walking on the lake bottom. It must have only been thirty feet deep. The giant made small foamy waves as they approached the distant shore. "I can't believe it's working. Well done, Grey Cloak."

With Gunder Island falling behind him, he looked forward to better days. Certainly the Sky Riders would be mad, but it wasn't right to keep him prisoner. And even though he'd agreed to it, he should have been able to come and go as he pleased.

Sure, they'll miss me, but I won't miss them. Well, not all of them. He would miss Anya, Stayzie, and Mayzie. After all, they were gorgeous. Yuri, not so much, but he was grateful that she'd taught him how to use wizardry. The men weren't bad, but he hadn't warmed to their brusque manner, either. They were all obsessed with Black Frost. Frankly, he was tired of hearing about it.

Tontor took long and easy steps as he churned forward at a steady pace. It made for a gentle ride, and Grey Cloak could dip his toes in the water. The trip became relaxing as they approached the shoreline of Valley Shire and its rich grasslands.

What am I going to do when I get there? His eyelids became heavy, and he yawned. He still needed to find Dyphestive and the members of Talon, but he had no idea how to find any of them. All that mattered was that he would be free. *I'll figure it out.*

He still had coins in his magic cloak's pocket, and he had a sword and a dagger and the Figurine of Heroes too. *Yeah, I'll be fine.*

A seagull as big as he had ever seen dropped out of the sky. It flapped its wings and squawked at him.

"Will you get away?" He shooed it with his arms. "I'm not your dinner. What are you doing flying at night, anyway?"

The bird let out an angry squawk, flapped its wings, and flew away.

"Finally, some peace and quiet. Long overdue, if I don't mind saying so myself." He covered his mouth and yawned. "I remember when I used to never be tired. Perhaps I'll find a very nice inn and rest."

The distant shoreline was closing in. Tontor was moving a lot quicker than he'd realized. His great strides had covered half the distance quite fast. At the rate they were going, they would make it to the shore within an hour.

"I can't believe it!" He stretched out his arms and pumped his fists. "It's good to be me."

Over the next hour, his tired eyes became bright. He

couldn't wait to kiss the ground on the other side. All of a sudden, they were right on top of the sandy shores of Valley Shire.

Tontor's head emerged from the lake, then his waist. Water ran down the giant's body. "I told you that I could do it." He took a deep breath through his wide nostrils. "Tontor tall and strong."

"Tontor, you are amazing!" He climbed down to the giant's shoulder. The rising sun shone in his eyes as he squinted and scanned the shoreline. He jumped off Tontor and splashed feetfirst into the water. Kicking out his bare feet, he raced to the shore. He ran up the sandy bank to where the green grass waited and fell to his knees and kissed it. "I did it, I did it, I did it."

He rolled onto his back and breathed in the cool morning air deeply. His eyes were closed, and he enjoyed having the sun on his face. A moment later, a shadow fell over him. "I can't thank you enough, Tontor. You are a true friend."

Tontor didn't reply. He rose on his elbows and opened his eyes, blinking. Anya and Cinder were on the beach and looking right at him.

Anya had a smirk on her face as she asked, "Did you enjoy your trip?"

Grey Cloak rose and asked, "How did you find me?"

"We knew you left," Anya said. She was striking in her armor with the wind blowing through her hair. "Honestly, I'm surprised it took so long for you to take off."

"Surprised? You mean you wanted me to leave?"

"We anticipated it. After all, all you did was complain about the training."

"But Hammerjaw was sleeping, and the rest of you weren't around. How in the infernos did you find me?"

"I could see you," Cinder said with a nod. "It wasn't difficult. It never is, for me."

"Of course, Hammerjaw doesn't sleep, either. His eyes might be closed and his nose full of snores, but I assure you, he's quite alert." She was cradling her helmet under her arm, but she put it on her head. "Come on now."

He shook his head. "I'm not going back."

"You gave your word."

"It wasn't a blood oath. Besides…" He glanced at Tontor. The giant was sneaking up behind Cinder. The dragon's eyes slid to look at him. "I was only helping my new friend Tontor." He smiled proudly. "We came ashore to retrieve some butter."

"Budder," Tontor said. "Tontor want budder. Good on crab." The giant tackled Cinder's face and locked his hands on the dragon's horns. They wrestled and tugged back and forth over the sand. Tontor grunted and growled loudly. Cinder flipped his head upward and tossed Tontor through the air. Tontor landed on his backside. He jumped up and came running back at Cinder. "Do it again!"

Grey Cloak and Anya moved away from the two towering titans and into the grass.

"You sure know how to pick your friends," she said with her gaze on the monstrous brutes. "I have to hand it to you."

"He's been better company than the rest of you so far," he replied.

Cinder was on his hind legs, pushing against Tontor, battling with all of his might. The dragon used his massive tail and flipped Tontor off his feet.

Tontor jumped up and said, "You stop doing that, Alligator Arms!"

Cinder stiffened and looked at his claws.

Grey Cloak and Anya burst out in laughter. As soon as she looked away, he started to run, but she caught him by the hood of his cloak.

"Certainly, you now know that you can't escape."

He held his thumb and forefinger close together and said, "I was this close."

"No, you weren't."

"I think I was. I think that you got lucky."

She shook her head. "Luck had nothing to do with it. But I have to hand it to you—using the giant to get across was impressive, just not impressive enough."

They stood side by side, watching the giant and the dragon wrestle and play like a boy and his oversize dog. They rolled over the sand and on top of one another. Tontor's efforts to pin Cinder down were futile. The dragon slipped or broke free of the giant's iron grip every time.

"Cinder!" Anya called. "It's time to go."

The dragon had the giant pinned down in the sand with his front claws. "Alligator Arms. I ought to roast you." He moved toward Anya.

Tontor rolled up on his knees and said, "What about my budder? I want budder!"

Grey Cloak approached his towering friend and gazed up into his eyes. "Tontor, I promise you that I will get you budder... I mean butter, as soon as she lets me." He stabbed a finger in Anya's direction.

Tontor gave a big, crooked frown and glared at Anya.

"She steal my budder. Tontor don't like her. Don't like her at all. Next time he might eat her." He turned his back and walked into the water. "Goodbye, Grey Cloak. Don't break your promise. That make Tontor mad."

Anya stood shoulder to shoulder with Grey Cloak and said, "Well, that was stupid."

"What was?" he asked.

"You made a giant a promise. If you don't keep it, he'll find you, rip your arms out of their sockets, then eat you."

"Ha-ha," he deadpanned.

She gave him a serious look. "I'm not kidding."

As Tontor vanished into the water, Grey Cloak swallowed.

39

Once again, Grey Cloak found himself sitting behind Anya and flying through the air on Cinder. He had his hand wrapped around her waist and was resting his face on her back. It would be a short trip back to Gunder Island, but a catnap would do him some good.

"Excuse me, but what do you think you are doing?"

He kept his eyes closed and nuzzled her back as he mumbled, "Resting."

"I don't think so. It's morning. Time for training."

"Come on, Anya, can't you cut me some slack? Only this once. I'm tired."

She pushed back into him. "You should have thought about that before you departed in the middle of the night."

The steady beating of Cinder's wings lifted them higher

into the air. He bent his neck back toward them and said, "I beg your pardon, Anya, but where are we going?"

"The sky is yours, Cinder. But keep our flight gentle. I have some training to conduct."

"As you wish." The dragon soared high above Lake Flugen and angled toward the rising sun.

Grey Cloak yawned. "Training, huh? What sort of training can we do up here?" He perked up. "Wait, are you going to let me fly Cinder?"

"In your dreams," she said. "Besides, Cinder flies himself."

"You can say that again," Cinder said.

"Cinder is a grand dragon, ancient, not like most of the others. Most dragons, called middlings, are the sort that you'll learn to ride. They are smaller and more like horses. Those, you do need to learn how to fly and master. Master them, and maybe, one day, you'll have a grand dragon like Cinder." She patted one of Cinder's horns. "Of course, he's one of a kind."

"No doubt," Cinder said.

"Ah, so if I'm not going to learn to fly a dragon, then what are we going to do?"

"This." Anya leaned over the saddle, which was a well-crafted attachment made from well-worn chestnut leather. It was fitted with several large pouches used for storage. It also held sheaths filled with extra swords and daggers, not to mention an oversize quiver that held four-foot-long javelins. It was the javelins that she reached for. She handed one to Grey Cloak and grabbed another one for herself.

Grey Cloak ran his dexterous fingers over the polished blackwood of the javelin. It was as smooth as glass, and he could barely feel the wood grain in the shaft. He had plenty of experience making weapons in Rhonna's forge back in Havenstock. That included making spears and hunting javelins. He knew a good craft when he saw it. "Who makes these?"

"I do," she said. "I'm quite the woodworker. A natural. The wood is harvested in Hidemark's forest. It's very serviceable."

He spun the well-balanced javelin in his hand. "What good is a stick of wood against, well, a dragon?"

She turned all the way around in her saddle and faced him with the javelin lying across her lap. "You've spent a lot of time training with Yuri, correct?"

He nodded.

"Now it is time to raise your wizardry to the next level." She lifted the javelin with one hand and held it before his eyes. Her hand started to glow with a fiery-orange hue, and the shaft of wood began to vibrate. Pulsating energy expanded from the middle and spread rapidly to the ends. The long projectile pulsated with magic. "I call it the javelin of thunder. Now you try it."

"Me?" He brought his javelin around to his chest. He'd

never tried to harness his magic into another item before. "There's a first time for everything." He summoned his power. The magic started in his chest and flowed through his body. His heartbeat pushed it into his arms and hands.

"Don't force it," Anya said. "Remember, it's not supposed to erupt out of you as you've been trained but to fill the weapon instead."

Grey Cloak's energy flooded through his hands and into the shaft.

"Not so fast!" Anya warned.

The javelin burned white hot and exploded with a loud *zap-crack* and broke in the middle. Both ends were smoking and charred, and one of the charred ends caught fire.

He eyed the javelin then Anya and said, "I can mend it."

"Don't worry about it," she said. "It happens."

"Did the same thing happen to you the first time?"

"No." She turned around in the saddle and said, "Cinder, take us down. I need a target."

"As you wish," the dragon said. He leaned right into a graceful dive. In seconds, they were skimming the top of the lake and flying toward the beach. An abandoned, rotting dock was covered in seabirds, which scattered the moment they saw the dragon coming.

Anya hurled her javelin at the dock. The missile sailed like a streak of lightning, flying true, and hit the dock. The dock then exploded into splinters of wood.

Cinder veered away, turned upward, and flew back into the sky.

"Impressive," Grey Cloak said. He liked what he saw. If he could do that, then it would add another weapon to his arsenal. He reached for another javelin.

Anya grabbed his hand. Hers was trembling. "Don't overdo it. A day at a time. Pulling the magic will drain you."

"Is that why your hand is shaking?"

She jerked it away. "No."

He held out his hand. It was as steady as a rock. Yuri had trained him to exhaustion before, until his limbs would tremble, so it made sense if that was the case with Anya. If it wasn't the magic that affected her, then it could have been something else. "Is there something wrong that you aren't telling me about?"

With her face forward, she said, "No. There's nothing abnormal about a tremble after the wizardry runs through your fingers."

"If you say so."

"Anya," Cinder said with his head tilted downward, "I see trouble."

She stood up in her stirrups and peered in the same direction that Cinder was looking. Grey Cloak did the same.

A league away from Valley Shire's lakeshore were many black plumes of smoke. In the smoke were charred remains of buildings. It looked like the entire hillside had been set on fire.

"Shall we take a closer look?" Cinder asked, his gaze moving from side to side.

"Yes," Anya answered as she grabbed a javelin, "but keep an eye out for dragons."

Every building of the small town had been burned to the ground, reduced to ash. The stonework was black. A few chimneys were still standing, but almost everything was knocked down or decimated by fire.

Grey Cloak walked through the smoking remains. His eyes watered and burned. The dirt was black and covered in ash. His nose twitched as he smelled vinegar and brimstone. He came upon a dead body, one of hundreds. The skin and muscles had been burned from a child's body. Nothing was left but white bone. His heart sank.

"Hickory," Anya said as she walked over to him. She was carrying a javelin and used it to turn over a slab of wood that half-covered another dead body.

"Pardon?" he asked.

"That's the smell of burned red oak—vinegar. It burns

slowly and is excellent firewood. This entire village is made of it." She squatted and looked at the skeleton with its mouth open. "They had no chance. The attack came without warning."

Grey Cloak noticed that he was standing beside a large paw print in the ground. "Riskers?"

She nodded and took her helmet off. "That's the print of a middling dragon. There were more than one."

He had never witnessed such devastation before. The dead were scattered as far as the eye could see. All of the livestock were burned. The crops were destroyed. "Are you telling me that they killed all of these people? Hundreds? For what reason?"

"To send a message," Anya said in a grim tone. "To us." She took a deep breath. "They are becoming bolder, it seems."

"What do you mean by that?"

"Black Frost wants to draw us out. He knows that the Sky Riders are bound to serve the greater good of Gapoli. This is what he does. He taunts us."

"Are you telling me that he's done this before?"

Anya gave him a disappointed look. "This is exactly what we have been telling you about. Black Frost and his army are evil." She spread her hands out. "This is how he operates. Serve him or die. And every so often, make an example by burning alive a bunch of innocent people." She spiked her helmet on the ground like a ball. "This is why we fight!"

For the first time in his life, Grey Cloak was numb all over. The truth began to seep in as he imagined all of the screams of the terrified people. He was witnessing what had been destined to be his future. Young boys and girls like him, raised to become dragon-riding murderers. If he had not escaped, he would have been involved in the destruction. The innocent blood of hundreds would have covered his hands. And Dyphestive's.

"I'm ashamed," he said. He walked over and picked up her helmet. "I was almost a part of this."

Anya took it from him and said, "I hope you are beginning to understand why Black Frost must be destroyed. His provocations will become bolder. He wants to drag every last one of us into the open. But this one is too close to home. We must tell the others."

"Who is going to bury all of these people?"

"This town has neighbors. Eventually, when their fear subsides and the coast is clear, they will take care of it." She put her helmet on and headed toward Cinder. The dragon was sitting on a nearby rise, watching the land like a hawk. "There is nothing that they can do now. Fortunately, no flesh left for the vultures to pick clean. The corpses will be undisturbed."

Grey Cloak caught up with her and looked over his

shoulder. "If the Riskers did this to bait us, wouldn't it be possible that they might still be around?"

"If that were the case, Cinder would have spotted them. Dragon fire burns a long time. This attack happened over a day ago. Given the circumstances, I think that this was a message." She climbed the rope ladder that led to Cinder's saddle. "Hurry."

Grey Cloak followed suit and took his place behind her.

"Let's go, Cinder. Ride the sky," she said.

Cinder's muscular legs bunched up under him, and he launched into the air. Grey Cloak's stomach dropped down into his toes. *I'll never get used to that.* In a matter of seconds, they were flying straight toward Gunder Island.

Grey Cloak took a lasting look at the village behind him. Gray-black smoke hung like a cloud of death over it. Sadness mixed with anger filled his heart. As they passed over the shoreline and rose to new height, he noticed the large sand dunes starting to move. He stiffened.

What is that?

Black wings burst free of the sand. A dragon's head and long neck popped out. Sand slid down the scales of its body, and a rider in plate armor was revealed.

Grey Cloak started hitting Anya on the back with his hand. "Anya! We have company!"

"I beg your pardon?"

He grabbed her head and twisted it around. "There!"

Three dragons with riders, Riskers, burst free of the

sands and soared toward Cinder's streaming tail. The riders aimed bows with glowing arrows. Their full helmets hid their faces but had small openings for their eyes.

"Company, Cinder! Company!" Anya shouted. "Go higher and away from Gunder."

"Away from Gunder?" Grey Cloak asked. "But we need help!"

"We can't risk revealing Hidemark to the enemy." She pulled a javelin free of the quiver and charged it with power then handed it to Grey Cloak. "How's your aim?" she asked as she grabbed another and charged it too.

"We're about to find out." He twisted around in the saddle, cocked the javelin back, and slung it at the Risker in the center of the pack.

The dragon turned easily out of the missile's path, and it passed yards away from the dragon's wing.

"Apparently, my aim needs some work."

The Riskers let their arrows fly, and the missiles rocketed toward Cinder's haunches.

Cinder took a hard turn to the left and kept barrel-rolling. Two arrows slipped under him, but the third exploded into his backside, and he bucked.

Grey Cloak was thrown from the saddle, and he began free-falling toward the lake, over a thousand feet down. "Horseshoes!"

<h1 style="text-align:center">41</h1>

I should have stayed in bed. With less than a thousand feet between him and the lake, Grey Cloak twisted and turned in the air. He didn't fear the water, but he knew the impact would kill him. With the choppy blue-green waters rushing up to meet him, he remembered falling into the chasm at Lovers' Gorge. He grabbed the edges of his cloak. *Slow down. Slow down.* The cloak billowed outward. His rapid descent almost slowed to a stop as he floated downward.

"Ya-hah!" He pumped his fist. "Yes!" Suddenly, the lake waters didn't look so terrifying. He felt so light that he could have sworn he could walk on them. He peered upward.

Cinder and Anya were jetting through the sky. It looked like Anya was throwing bolts of lightning from the dragon's back. The Riskers were returning fire with magic-charged arrows of power. The bright volleys went back and forth.

"Huh?" Grey Cloak only saw two dragons. They were only middling dragons, little more than half the size of Cinder. Anya must have taken out the third dragon. "Well done, Anya. That was quick."

A dragon roared.

Grey Cloak twisted around in midair. A Risker was making a beeline toward him, and the dragon's jaws were wide open.

"Gaaaah!" *Fall down! Fall down! Fall down!*

His cloak closed, and he dropped like a stone. The dragon whizzed right over his head, missing him by inches. It let out a disappointed shriek and banked hard right in the air with its neck twisted all the way around. Grey Cloak plummeted toward the lake back first and looking skyward. The dragon zeroed in on him again.

He craned his neck around. He was only a few seconds from death. *Slow down. Slow down.*

The cloak spread out its folds like a living thing, and his rapid free fall became a slow descent.

The dragon came right at him. Its jaws were opened wide and glowing with volcanic fire.

With a quick glance downward, Grey Cloak realized only a couple hundred feet were left between him and the water. But it was hard to guess for certain over such an expansive area.

The dragon closed in. Fire erupted from its mouth. Grey Cloak dropped like an anchor. He felt every bit of the heat from the fire on his face. Those roasting flames were soon to be cooled by the lake waters.

The dragon let out another angry shriek. Its rider craned his neck and shook his fist. While falling through the air, Grey Cloak waved. *Missed me.* The wind whistled by his ears. *Zooks! Stop falling! Stop—*

He smacked back-first into the water. *Splash!*

ARROWS EXPLODED into Cinder's backside, rattling the huge dragon's scales. He flinched underneath the saddle. "Are you going to kill them, or do I have to?" he bellowed.

"I'm trying!" Anya had lost sight of Grey Cloak, and she'd been hurling javelin after javelin ever since he fell. Only one javelin had connected so far. It was lodged in a middling dragon's chest. They were quick in the air and flew in jagged patterns. She charged up one more javelin, tapping the reserves of her power, and slid her neck to the side. A glowing arrow streaked by her head. She aimed and hurled the javelin.

The Risker anticipated the throw and pulled the reins on his dragon to the left. The dragon veered right into the missile path. It lodged in the dragon's neck and exploded. Dragon and warrior spiraled downward.

Anya bellowed in triumph. "Victory!" She'd taken a guess that the dragon would veer left, fooling the rider and connecting. That left only one dragon to battle, that she could see.

Seeing that she was almost out of javelins, the Risker snapped his reins like a rider on a horse. The dragon's wings beat faster, and it soared over Cinder. A stream of flame spewed out of the dragon's mouth toward Cinder's back.

"Dive, Cinder! Dive!"

Cinder dropped just as the hot flames licked Anya's face, and the searing dragon flames heated her helmet. The Riskers dove after them. Cinder could take the smaller dragon in a straight flight, but he couldn't outmaneuver the middling in midair.

Anya leaned forward and yelled, "I'm almost out of javelins. What do you want to do?"

"I have a plan," the dragon said calmly. He flew low, over the lake, creating waves behind him. His eyes scanned the water. "Find a way to keep that dragon off of my tail, if you will."

The Risker bore down on them, firing arrow after arrow. Anya grabbed her last javelin. She didn't have any more power to charge it, but she could still throw it like a champ. "Take this!" She gritted her teeth and threw it.

The javelin sailed true. The Risker didn't even veer

away. The javelin ricocheted harmlessly off of the dragon's snout.

"Cinder!" Anya called. "Whatever you are coming up with, you'd better come up with it soon. I'm running out of ideas!" She unhooked a pendant-shaped shield that was hanging from the saddle and hid behind it. Arrow after arrow exploded into the shield, jolting her arms with lancing pain. "That Risker is good!"

Her dragon swept over the water. Anya had no idea what he was doing.

The next arrow hit her shield dead center. She recoiled backward, and her feet loosened in the stirrups. Bracing for the next impact, she asked, "How many bloody arrows do you have?" Out of the corner of her eye, she saw the third dragon she'd lost track of zeroing in. She ducked, but the third dragon's talons hit her hard and knocked her out of the saddle.

42

Pain exploded through every part of Grey Cloak's back as he sank into the water. Getting run over by a stampeding bull wouldn't have felt any worse. He'd never imagined that water could feel so hard. *Ouch!*

He floated in the deep-green water, numb all over, as he gathered his senses. Instinctively, he opened his eyes. The water wasn't clear, and they burned. Though he could see daylight, he was still sinking. He swam upward with all of his might, but the fall had taken the wind out of him. His lungs quickly began to burn.

He inched upward, but his clothing was dragging him down, so he unhooked his sword belt and dropped it. A large silver fish passed right by his eyes. Its scales shimmered like a hazy sun. Like a frog, he swam upward, climbing through the chill water, his tired arms straining with the effort. He went toward the light, and his head burst out above the waves.

He sucked in huge gulps of air as he treaded the water. He wiped the hair from his eyes.

Where's that dragon?

He spun in the water, his head twisting from left to right. Though the sun was in his eyes, he saw the dragon coming straight for him. A stream of flame shot out of its mouth right toward him.

Grey Cloak sank into the water as the flames roared just over his head, licking the lake water, which started to boil. He swam down deeper. The dragon hovered above, blasting out another stream of fire that burrowed a sizzling hole in the lake. It created a vortex of boiling water that spun and churned around it.

Thunderbolts! He swam like a frog as fast as his arms and legs would move. The churning water pulled him back toward the underwater pillar of flame. The tips of his toes inched into the vortex, which caught his feet like a hook and sucked him in. He spun round and round like he was being whipped through the wind. He had no control over his body. He was a ship tossed and turned by an all-powerful sea. *I'm going to die.*

With his eyes open and the water tearing at his eyelids, he could see his body nearing the dragon's flame. If he didn't drown first, it would soon be over instantly when he hit the flame.

The quicker, the better.

The water boiled around him. He wanted to scream from the growing pain. Something huge stirred the water, and the dragon flame died, the waters no longer swirling. Using his last ounce of strength, Grey Cloak half-swam, half-floated to the top. He gulped in air the moment his face emerged from the water.

The dragon was shrieking like a banshee at a water giant who had risen out of the water. The giant was a beastly brute, more so than Tontor. It hurled a boulder at the dragon, and the dragon and the Risker flew away.

Grey Cloak fought to keep his buoyancy above the choppy waves caused by the giant's arrival, and he bobbed up and down in the water. He was exhausted. His feet paddled with every ounce of strength he had left, though it was failing and his clothing was weighing him down.

Don't sink. Don't sink. Don't sink.

The giant was a bald brute with shoulders as wide as a small ship. When the giant turned around, his wake washed over Grey Cloak, and his body blocked the sun. If he noticed the small elf treading in the water, he didn't show it. The giant cast a glance over his shoulder and slowly sank back into the water.

Grey Cloak panted. He had only one thing in mind as he tried to swim toward the far-distant shore. *Don't drown.*

43

The third dragon had come out of nowhere and knocked Anya clean out of her saddle. Her fingers clawed for purchase as she slid down from Cinder's saddle, and she hooked her hand in a stirrup and held on for dear life. "Guh!" she groaned as she tried to pull herself back up.

Cinder was flying fast over the lake in a zigzag pattern. Her toes were almost skimming the water. An arrow whizzed by her. "I hate Riskers!"

She watched the water rush underneath her feet. "Cinder, what are you do—"

A giant face was underneath the waves. The flat-faced giant exploded out of the water. He missed Cinder's tail by several yards and grabbed the Risker's dragon by the feet.

The dragon put up a fight. Fire streamed out of his snout into the giant's face. The massive giant wrapped his arms around the dragon's neck and pulled the dragon and man into the depths of the lake.

"I hope that was your plan!" Anya called as she started climbing her way back into the saddle.

"Of course it was," Cinder said confidently. He turned right and headed skyward.

Anya caught sight of the last Risker, the one that had knocked her out of the saddle. They were fleeing north. "Don't let them get away!"

"I won't!" Cinder beat his powerful wings fast and hard, closing the gap quickly.

The Risker fired an arrow that exploded off of Cinder's skull, but the dragon didn't slow. He caught up to the middling dragon, bit down on its tail, and shook it like a dog.

The middling dragon shrieked then turned its neck toward Cinder and spit flame at him.

With his face in the fire, Cinder barrel-rolled and twisted the dragon. The middling dragon's body bent in an awkward position under Cinder. Performing his signature move, Cinder locked his talons on one of the dragon's wings and ripped it off. The middling dragon let out an earsplitting shriek that would send villagers a league away running for their lives. Cinder drove the dragon toward the ground and crashed it into the beach.

Anya jumped out of her saddle a split second before

Cinder landed. But she wasn't alone in her efforts. So did the Risker.

The middling and Cinder squared off. The smaller dragon sank low to the ground and hissed. The one-winged monster had murder lurking in its burning-yellow eyes. It jumped at Cinder claws first, ripping into the scales covering his body.

Cinder roared and struck. His mighty jaws chomped down on the dragon's serpentine neck and closed like a vise. Flames blasted out of the middling's wriggling snout. It twisted and thrashed violently. Cinder slung the dragon around like a rag, and his final throw snapped the middling's neck. The flames in the dragon's mouth went out, and the glow in its eyes died.

Anya was standing a fair distance away from the Risker. Out of respect, they'd watched the dragons battle before they did. The Risker turned to face her. The man was wearing a suit of armor that was fashioned similarly to hers. The only difference was his helmet. Hers was open-faced, and his fully covered his face above the mouth.

"Shall we battle, the two of us, or are you going to have your dragon eat me?" the man asked in a charming voice.

Anya pulled her sword out of its sheath. "You can always surrender."

"Ha," the Risker said as he removed his longsword from his sheath. "That won't be happening. So I take it that I'll fight you and not the dragon."

"No doubt you deserve to be incinerated by Cinder's flames, but that would be too merciful. I'm going to make you pay for what you and your vile ilk did to all of those innocent people."

The Risker cut his sword through the air. "Cinder, huh?" He glanced back at the dragon, who was dragging his victim into the water. "So you must be Anya."

"I am."

"My name is Blackstone." He took off his helmet and tossed it aside. He was in his thirties and handsome, with jet-black hair and ice-blue eyes. "I was a friend of your parents."

She took off her helmet and dropped it in the sand. "You were no friend of my parents if you serve Black Frost."

"You are very beautiful, like your mother. I hated to see her killed. But she put up a valiant fight on the Day of Betrayal. It was a sad thing to see her die."

Anya's eyebrows knitted. Blackstone was smug and cocky. Clearly a natural. "You are scum."

"Tell me, Anya, when I win, will the almighty Cinder avenge you, or will he become a mount for me? I could use a dragon like him. Aside from Black Frost, he is without rival."

"You aren't going to beat me," she said.

"Funny. That's the same thing that your mother said."

Anya's rage boiled over. She charged Blackstone and thrust.

Blackstone swatted her sword aside. His blade glowed with inner fire. He parried away her next two strikes and backpedaled. "You fight well. Your mother would be proud." He parried again and countered with quick underhand swing that nicked her left eyelid. "Not well enough."

Anya jumped backward. Blood trickled from her wound. She was seething. There she was, face-to-face with one of Black Frost's servants, who had admitted to killing her mother. And she was blowing it. *Settle yourself, Anya. Settle!*

"Are we finished? Do you surrender? It would be wise if you did," he said as he tugged on the long hairs of his mustache.

She held her sword with both hands, and the wings on the pommel started to glow and shimmer. Her sword energized her body. "Stifle your worm tongue and fight!"

"As you wish," Blackstone said nonchalantly. He attacked with a whirlwind of overhand chops that sent Anya backpedaling and jumping from side to side.

In moments, Blackstone proved to be the best fighter she had ever faced, and she wasn't ready. She parried for her life. His sword tip clipped at the hard ridges of her arm.

"I'm going to peel that shell off of you one plate at a time, woman," Blackstone said as he took on a vicious demeanor. "Your dragon and your head will be mine. Black Frost will raise me up for it!"

Anya ducked under a sword chop that would have

taken her head from her shoulders. She jumped and rolled over on her side then came up to a knee, raising her sword in a split second. The magic swords clashed, and sparks flew all over. She leg-swept Blackstone, and he fell onto his backside.

She jumped on top of him, and they rolled over the ground, wrestling for their lives. Blackstone had quickly proved he was a better swordsman, seasoned, crafty, and strong. But Anya was buying time.

Blackstone head-butted her. "How did that feel?"

She head-butted him back harder, and his nose pressed into his skull. "How did *that* feel?"

He tore away from her, jumped up, and said, "You broke my nose, you red-haired witch. I have to admit, you have more fire than your mother did." He twisted his sword through the air. "It will make this conquest all the more enjoyable."

Taking labored breaths, Anya firmed her stance in the sand. She held her sword with trembling arms in the low-guard position called plow and eyed Blackstone. He was bigger and better, and he knew it. She was weaker and less experienced. And that was exactly what she wanted him to think. She had one chance before she died. "Go ahead. Finish me."

Blackstone moved like a gazelle and sped toward her. His sword shining like the sun, he thrust. She returned the thrust with all she had.

Blades pierced armor and the bodies underneath. Anya screamed. Blackstone's sword went straight through the meat of her shoulder. The Risker looked down at her with triumph in his eyes. But that moment of glory faded when his gaze dropped down and he saw her sword buried in his chest. It had gone straight through his heart. He gasped, sobbed miserably, his chin quivering, and died.

She stood, Blackstone's sword still sticking out of her shoulder, and staggered toward Cinder, who was coming her way. Her vision blurred, and she passed out in the sand.

44

Grey Cloak was lying with the side of his face in the sand and the hot sun on his back. The waves crashed on the shore, the water washing over his toes. He was exhausted. How he'd made it back to the shore, he didn't know. He didn't even remember swimming. If anything, he only remembered drowning.

He fought his way over to his back and stared at the clear sky. No dragons could be seen. He wasn't even sure what shore he was on—Gunder Island or Valley Shire. With a grunt, he forced himself up into a sitting positing. His body and clothing were covered in sand, and he was drenched. *Where's Anya?*

The last time he remembered seeing her, she had been battling the Riskers. But there was no sign of them. If she and Cinder had won the fight, certainly they would have come after him. It wasn't a good sign that they weren't around. A bad feeling formed in the pit of his stomach.

They couldn't have lost.

He fought to stand. That was when he realized that he was back on Gunder Island. He took off his cloak and shook the sand off. The gray cloak was bone dry once he waved it. The rest of his clothing was soaked. *That's interesting.*

He checked the many pockets inside the lining and fished out a few coins then put them back. The Figure of Heroes was secure too. He'd managed to escape with his life and his most prized possessions. The only things he'd lost were his belt and his sword. *Easy come, easy go. Not my style, anyway.*

Grey Cloak stared out over the great pond. He saw no sense in trying to cross it again. For the time being, he would just as soon avoid the water. The more important thing was finding Anya. He was worried, and he still saw no sign of her.

When he began his trek toward the forest jungle, a shadow fell over his shoulder, and he turned to look skyward.

Justus and his dragon, Firestok, landed behind him. "Grey Cloak, come with me. Hurry," Justus said, sounding heavyhearted.

Grey Cloak did as he was told and climbed onto the dragon's saddle. "What's wrong? Did something happen to Anya?"

"Hold tight," Justus said as Firestok lifted off. "It's bad, my friend. Anya was mortally wounded. She's dying."

45

DARK MOUNTAIN

The place was called the Long Road. It was leagues of wide road hewn out of the black rock and leveled off, and it led to the civilization cradled in Dark Mountain. The Long Road started at the base of the mountain range and curved up into the platform of rock's great heights. It was the only way into Dark Mountain and the only way out, unless you were flying on a dragon.

Rhonna was sitting on an overlook, watching the Long Road from a far distance. The muscles between her shoulder blades tensed. She'd traveled a lot in Gapoli over the decades and had lived in six of the nine major territories, but she'd never been so far north in Ugrad. It was a cold, dark, and hard place, and she had been born and raised in Dwarf Skull, arguably the toughest place in the world.

"What's on your mind?" Lythlenion asked. He was sitting on a dry bed of grass beside her, eating wild nuts. "Or should I not ask?"

"Look at those troops along the Long Road. There must be thousands," she said as she looked through a spyglass. Every hundred yards was a stone watchtower, and troops were staggered along both sides of the road. "No one is going to get in and out of there unless they let you."

Bowbreaker was standing on a bluff just below Rhonna and Lythlenion, casually leaning on his longbow. "I've counted over three hundred towers and estimate five thousand soldiers that guard the Long Road. There is a checkpoint every half league. Even so, plenty of merchants and travelers are still coming and going, as you can see. I think they like to see the dragons, and Black Frost likes to show them off. The people pay him homage like he's some sort of god."

"Figures," Rhonna puffed on her cigar. Dark Mountain might as well have been the jaws of death to an enemy trapped within. If Dyphestive was alive and in there, she felt he would never come back out. She cared for the stripling, felt responsible for what had happened to him, and wished she were going in there instead of Zora, but that wasn't the plan. "We should go look for him," she muttered.

"Ah, you're still wrestling with that, are you?" Lythlenion asked as he packed his nuts back into a small pouch he was carrying. "You have to have faith in our friends and stick with the plan. That's what you always say."

"I don't need you to remind me of that," she said as she blew smoke out of her nose. "I've told you time and again, Zora and Tanlin don't have my full trust. They are thieves. Now, they're running alongside a stinking sorceress with ties to a Minotaur and a jabbering swordsman. You want me to have faith in those people?"

"You didn't care for me much when we met," Lythle-nion pointed out.

"Me, either," Bowbreaker said.

"That was different," she said quietly.

Lythlenion reached over and rocked her shoulder. "Face it—you don't like anyone at all when you first meet them. It takes time for them to earn your trust. I don't blame you, but as for me personally, I like them, even though I don't know that Minotaur and blade master so much."

She stood up and let out an exaggerated "Well, gooood for you," and marched away.

At the bottom of the hill, Zora, Tanlin, Tatiana, Razor, and Grunt were waiting. They'd set up a camp half a league from the main road. "Well, where is this merchant who you've been telling us so much about?" she asked Tanlin.

"I'm certain that he'll be arriving soon," Tanlin assured her.

Rhonna noticed Tatiana staring at her. "What?"

"I was wondering if I could have a word," Tatiana said politely.

"It seems like a lot of you are full of words this morning. Why not you too? Spit it out."

"Privately?" Tatiana replied.

Rhonna sighed. She followed the sorceress away from the others but not before she heard Razor say to Grunt, "She is nothing like I envisioned. Not at all. I figured her for a strikingly beautiful brunette without a single crease in her face."

She glared back at him. Razor hid behind Grunt, who gave an animallike chuckle.

Tatiana faced her. "Rhonna, I want to apologize. I shouldn't have shoved myself in and you out like I did. It was rude and disrespectful of me."

"Is that it?"

Tatiana's fingers needled the air at her sides. She opened her mouth and closed it again. "No, that's not it. I thought that it might be wise to ask you if you would want to colead the group with me."

"Colead." Rhonna blew smoke up in the air. "That's a novel suggestion. Who else is going to colead this group with us? The Minotaur?"

"No, only us. Listen, you are a natural leader, and I'm learning, but the Wizard Watch insisted that I do what I am doing. I'm not trying to step on your toes, Rhonna. I'm only trying to do what needs to be done."

"Uh-huh." She tapped the ashes off of her cigar and ground them into the dirt with her toe. "I've fought for a lot of different people in my lifetime. Dwarves, men, orcs, and elves, and I know the difference between a good leader and a bad one."

"Am I a bad one?"

"No, you aren't a leader at all. Not so far as I can see." She turned and walked away, leaving Tatiana wide-eyed and with her jaw hanging.

46

"You are sure that this trip will be safe, Crane?" Tanlin asked.

"I never said that," Crane replied. He was sitting at the front of a horse-drawn wagon. Crane was a portly, well-dressed merchant who had curly brown hair and liked to wear purple and a lot of gold jewelry. "It's Dark Mountain. There's always an element of danger. But so long as you play by the rules, everything will turn out in your favor."

"We aren't playing by the rules. That's what worries me," Tanlin replied as he watched Zora take her place beside Crane.

The likable merchant said, "You don't have to take the trip if you don't want to."

Zora saw the deep creases building in Tanlin's face and said, "I'll be fine. You know that I can take care of myself."

"And I'll take care of her too," Crane said as he patted her leg. "Don't trouble yourself, Tanlin. No one you know knows their way around Dark Mountain better than me. I've been trading my silks there for decades."

"Oh, silk," Zora said as she looked back into the covered wagon. Bundles of silk were wrapped in cotton covers and bound with twine. "Anything that will fit me?"

"Everything will fit you," Crane said as he looked her over.

Tanlin made his way over to Zora's side of the wagon. "Be wary of him. He's a bit ornery."

Zora bent down and kissed Tanlin on the cheek. "I will." She took off her dagger belt and handed it over to him. "I guess I won't be needing this. Will you hold onto it for me?"

"You know that I will." Tanlin's eyes were watering when he said, "Goodbye. See you in a few weeks."

Crane leaned over and said, "A few months, you mean. I'll be back when my business is done in a week, but if all goes well, she won't be picked up until I can return again. Be patient, brother. These things take time, but your plan is a good one. I'll meet you back in Crack Scowl." He snapped the reins, and the horse pulled the wagon forward.

Zora waved goodbye to the company.

Lythlenion waved and said, "May my blessings go with you."

"You, too, Lythlenion!" she said, remembering that

Talon was about to embark on an adventure of its own. She hated that she wouldn't be accompanying them.

Rhonna didn't wave. Her arms were crossed, and her cigar was smoking.

Tatiana was all smiles. "Take care, little sister."

Zora sought Bowbreaker, but the handsome elf ranger was nowhere to be found. That left only Grunt, who didn't so much as look at her, and Razor, who waved at her with one of his many swords and winked.

"You have good friends. Be thankful for them," Crane said. "They are getting harder and harder to come by these days."

The wagon churned along the bumpy Long Road and joined a long line of travelers who were coming and going. It was a steady stream of hundreds of people from all the lands as far at the eye could see. All of the known races of Gapoli were represented on the wide swath of road in one way or another. They were towing goods of all sorts in and out of Dark Mountain's inner city.

A pair of lizard men were driving an open wagon that was pulled by a lone ox south. The soldiers at the checkpoint towers along the road stopped the lizard men and searched their wagon. Every soldier was in uniform. They were wearing crimson tunics over chain-mail armor. Each of them was well equipped with spears in hand, sword and dagger on hip. A black mountain was embroidered on each of their chests. Higher up, soldiers were standing in the thirty-foot-high towers, crossbows in hand.

Crane slowly led the wagon by the search party. "Try not to stare," he said under his breath. "They don't like that."

Zora couldn't help but peek. Dark Mountain's soldiers were rough-handed men and women. They tore the lids off the barrels of the lizard men's wagon and plunged their hands into them. The lizard men were well-dressed, and their tongues flicked out of their mouths as they hissed in objection.

The end of a soldier's spear pressed against a lizard man's chest. He lifted his scaled hands in defeat.

"Do they always make searches like this?" Zora asked.

"Of course. No one enters or exits this hornet's nest without being searched at least a couple of times. The monarchs don't take chances. Don't worry—we'll be patted down as well. You'll get used to it after the first few times."

"Few times?"

He winked at her. "It's not so bad."

One of the soldiers standing in the lizard men's wagon removed a gold chalice from a barrel of grain. The olive-scaled lizard men paled, then they locked their fingers together and begged for mercy.

Dark Mountain's soldiers stormed the wagon. On the commanding sergeant's orders, the lizard men were dragged out of the wagon and slain on the spot with spears.

Spiders of ice ran down Zora's spine. "Did that just happen?" she asked, her breath visible in the chilly air.

"The soldiers of Dark Mountain are given a lot of liberty when it comes to dispensing their patented brand of justice. Do you know what they call them?"

"No," she said as she tightened a blanket over her shoulders.

"The Black Guard."

"Sounds terrible." Suddenly, her teeth were chattering.

"Don't worry, Zora. Keep your nose clean, and I'll get you back out of here. Believe me, I've been in and out of here a hundred times. You'll get used to it."

She looked back at the Black Guard. They were hauling the wagon and dragging the dead lizard men from the road. A feeling of dread overcame her. *I hope not.*

47

Crane's wagon was stopped five times on its trip up the Long Road. Dark Mountain's soldiers patted her down each time, but they only patted Crane down once.

"Don't take offense," he said to her. "They know me, but they don't know you."

"I would say some of them know me pretty well now," she said with disdain.

The Long Road came to an end in front of sheer cliffs that appeared to lead to nowhere. There was nothing but a vast mountain range that reached up into the clouds and stretched as far as the eye could see. The black peaks were snow-covered in some places. The surrounding volcanoes' orange glow cast wavering light on the mountainside.

With the wagon stopped, they faced a split in the cliff in

front of them. Travelers were moving along the road beyond the split and vanishing at the bend within.

Zora's heart began to pound. She had a curious nature about her and loved to travel. She'd even wanted to visit Dark Mountain, but now that she was facing its gloomy peaks up close, she wanted to turn back.

"It's not too late to change your mind," Crane said. He reached over and held her hand. "If you wish, I can conduct my business quickly, and we'll leave immediately, so as to not arouse suspicion."

"No, I can do this." She scanned the ridges. Dragons as big as horses were nestled like birds in the peaks. "What are they?"

"Drakes. Dragons, but not full-blooded. Many of them are wild, but like a good falcon, they can be trained."

A squad of Riskers jetted through the sky in a V formation. Armored soldiers rode on the dragons' backs between their great beating wings. The formation disappeared behind the hills. Another group followed, then two more.

Many people along the Long Road cheered. They took off their hats and waved them.

"The people here worship the Riskers. You'll have to get used to that. And be very careful what you say around those people," Crane warned as he flicked his whip stick. The wagon jerked forward.

Zora's hand tightly gripped Crane's. She liked the jolly

merchant, who always kept a warm smile on his face. "Have you ever seen him?"

"Who?"

"You know who."

"Ah," he said as he tilted his head back. "It's fine to mention his name here. They talk about him all the time. Like he's one of them. He's a dragon, after all. He likes it. Just don't say it too many times."

"Why?"

Crane chuckled. "He might show up. As for seeing Black Frost, no, I never have, but I've heard him. Believe me when I say that it is a sound you'll never forget." He continued, "They say he's enormous." He peered up at the tallest peak of the mountain range, which vanished in the clouds. "That it takes this entire mountain to hold him."

The horse-drawn wagon crossed over the giant split in the peaks, where the Long Road officially ended. Both sides of the split were under the guard of Dark Mountain's soldiers. They were posted on platforms of metalwork and wood that climbed fifty feet up. The expanse between the sides was over one hundred feet, and natural rock bridged the opening. It was heavily fortified, like a castle wall. A massive iron chain that was rolled up hung above them.

"I've seen that rolled down once," Crane commented. "It's an engineering marvel. Strong but flexible. No army could break it. Battering rams are futile against it. They call it the Iron Curtain."

She believed him. Soldiers at small posts were standing at the ready behind ballistae and other war-making devices. Many of the posts were hard to see, but everywhere she looked, she found one.

How in the world did Grey Cloak and Dyphestive get out of here? The Long Road was the only way in or out. The only other ways were to climb or fly. It might not be impossible, but from her vantage point, it looked so.

"Here we go," Crane said as he led the wagon around the first bend in the main road.

"Is that music?" she asked. Singing voices, the soft beating of drums, and the sound of string instruments being plucked could be heard everywhere. The sound wasn't bad, either. It was actually soothing.

"Yes. You'll hear it all of the time. Do you like it?"

Zora started to sway. "So far." She leaned forward, eyes wide. "Oh my."

Hidden on the other side of the sheer mountain walls was a city unlike any she'd ever been in. The ground was flat, and on that land were green fields surrounding a small city made out of the black rock that surrounded it. It was picturesque, in a dreary sort of way. Men and women were laboring in the fields. Barns and livestock fences could be seen in the distance.

She clung to Crane's arm when she saw the biggest ox she'd ever seen in a field nearby. It was ten feet tall at the shoulder. She pointed. "What in the world is that?"

"An ogre ox. Stupid and very gentle, but be sure that you don't walk behind them. Their farts will melt your face off."

Soaking her new surroundings in, she said, "I never would have imagined. This place is captivating."

Waterfalls cascaded from the cliffs, creating natural streams below. Herds of livestock were grazing. Farmers were wearing straw hats in the fields. Birds of all sizes and colors streaked through the sky and landed in the branches of the small trees and berry bushes.

The climate was warmer too. The cliffs shielded her from the mountains winds, and she felt a warm fog on her face. "It's cozy."

"Yes, the volcanoes make a very warm and fertile climate. It's like this all along the range both ways for leagues," he said.

"You mean this isn't the only city in Dark Mountain?"

"Lords no. There are many." He jabbed a finger in the air. "Some are higher in the peaks, and others dwell below. Marvelous, isn't it?"

"It feels wrong to say yes."

"Beauty is a great disguise for evil." He leaned into her. "But you didn't hear that from me."

48

Zora and Crane delivered the silks to several merchants spread throughout Dark Mountain. The cities had everything to offer that Raven Cliff did—tanners, blacksmiths, woodworkers, art shops, wine cellars, taverns, temples, and theaters. The streets were clean and the people well-kept and courteous but not overly friendly. The air tickled her nose, and it smelled like cherries from time to time.

The architecture varied from city to city. One was made up of small cottages, like something one would see in Westerlund's countryside. Another town was made up of wood buildings, much like Raven Cliff, and the larger town was made from blocks of slate that stacked up several stories high. They had no porches, only wooden doors that led from the cobblestone road straight into the buildings. The colorful awnings offered symbols of the business that was conducted inside.

As they moved on from city to city, delivering their goods, Zora said, "This place is huge. How in the world am I going to find Dyphestive?"

"Whatever you do, don't ask questions. You'll have to be very careful how you go about it. Look, learn, and listen. If anyone is suspected of spying, well..." Crane ran his finger across his throat. "They kill you first and ask questions later."

"Joy, joy."

"Let me show you something before we settle you in." He led the wagon higher up the winding streets. From the road, they could overlook the many cities in the valleys below. He came to a stop in front of a street that led straight up to beautiful castle-like buildings with tall spires, great balconies, and porches. A drop-down gate that blocked passage was manned by a score of soldiers. "That's where the monarchs of Dark Mountain live. Don't go there."

Her eyes ran up the road, which was paved with bricks of stone and something else. She gasped. "Is that gold brick?"

Crane nodded. "The monarchs enjoy showing off."

Gold bricks lined the street in zigzag patterns all of the way to the top of the monarchs' village.

"There must be thousands of them," she said with her eyes full of wonder.

"If that amazes you, imagine what it's like inside their castles." He turned the wagon around. "Come on. We need to get you registered and set you up with Deeann."

"Is Deeann part of the Brotherhood of Whispers?"

"No," he said flatly. "She's a fine businesswoman and a real taskmaster. Don't be fooling around. She'll put more on you."

"If you say so," Zora said. She couldn't help but cast her eyes everywhere at once. Something new was at every bend in the mountain—vineyards rich with burgeoning red and purple grapes, magnificent floral gardens, waterfalls, ponds, and hot springs. The citizens of Dark Mountain thrived in all of it. It gave her goose bumps all over. "I'm really having trouble understanding what is so bad about this place."

"Once you become a citizen, you can't leave here," he said. "The people have pledged their loyalty to Black Frost. Don't worry—you'll get the feel for it. Be careful, though. They'll sucker you in."

"If I'm to look for Dyphestive, where should I start? Will the Doom Riders walk the streets the same as everyone else?"

"Don't be surprised if you see the Riskers. They do walk the streets. As for the Doom Riders, well, I think they keep to themselves by the kennels."

She lifted an eyebrow. "Dog kennels?"

"No, dragon kennels. They sometimes refer to it as the

Hive. That's where they keep the dragons. I can't be certain, because I haven't been through all of Dark Mountain, but the kennels are in the higher places, closer to Black Frost." His gaze swept over the upper hills. "It won't be easy to get a peek up there, so be careful."

The wagon rolled back down the mountain and through the network of cities. Zora couldn't help but marvel at the thousands of people who thrived inside the mountain range—thousands she could see and tens of thousands that she couldn't. One could easily get lost in the vast place and never look back.

Crane led the wagon to a stop in front of a stone building with an awning that marked it as a tailor shop. It was one building among dozens that lined both sides of the busy street. "This city is called the Deuce, and it's where Deeann lives. You'll be staying here."

A halfling woman walked out of the front door. She was middle-aged and had long jet-black hair and walked with a wooden cane. She was wearing purple clothing and a tall hat with a brim. "Crane!" she said loudly. "I've been waiting for weeks for this shipment. Where have you been?"

He hopped out of the wagon and said in a voice full of charm, "Weeks, my butt. I'm weeks early."

"Huh!" Deeann had a gruffness about her. "Boys! Get out here and unload this wagon!"

Several halflings hustled out of the tailor shop and climbed into the wagon. All of them were strapping little men with curly hair and impish smiles. They formed a line from the wagon to the door and grabbed the packed-up silks, tossing them down the line, and in seconds, all of the sacks had disappeared inside the door. Then the halflings vanished behind them.

"I didn't say that it was all for you," Crane said to Deeann.

Deeann had a smirk on her face as she replied, "I didn't ask." She glanced up at Zora. "Who's this?"

"The help I promised. Deeann, this is Zora. Zora, this is Deeann."

Zora climbed out of the wagon and said, "Nice to meet you."

Deeann's eyes were as hard as chunks of coal. She reached out and touched Zora's hair and rubbed it in her fingers. "If you grow it longer, I can use it. Can you stitch?"

Zora nodded. "Stitch, sew, seam... you name it."

"Where are you from?"

"Raven Cliff."

Deeann nodded. "I have a tailor shop and a tavern. Can you serve?"

"Even a quarry gnome can serve."

Crane giggled.

Deeann took exception to Zora's remark and said, "Not in my kind of place!" She rubbed her dimpled chin and eyed her. "We work hard here, very hard. This place is nothing like anywhere else. So which is it, sew or serve?"

The halfling workers had their heads poked out of the front door. All of them had ornery looks on their faces. One of them winked at her.

"Both," Zora responded.

Deeann looked up at Crane and nodded. "I like her." She reached up and patted his belly. "That's more than I can say for you, Tubby."

49

Crane hung around for another week before he departed, but each day, Zora saw less and less of him. He hadn't been lying when he said that Deeann was a taskmaster. She kept after Zora all hours of the day, and Zora learned that the halflings were tireless workers. Even she had trouble keeping pace with them.

Deeann rotated Zora between the tailor shop and the tavern. She worked the tailor shop during the day and the tavern at night. She was a very popular barmaid with the patrons. They filled her ears with flattery and stories, and she laughed at their jokes as she served them.

It was the time in the tavern that benefitted her the most. People from all over the mountain came to Deeann's Tavern, which was known for fantastic sweetberry wine and cream-filled desserts. Her keen ears picked up on the goings on with the monarchs, Black Frost, and the Riskers. The people revered them and talked as if they would live forever under Black Frost's regime.

Before long, Zora had come to know her way around the mountain very well. Deeann had her make deliveries all over the network of cities. She used that time to figure out exactly where everyone was. One day, she made a delivery of uniforms to Riskers' Roost, a garrison high in the mountains, where the Riskers lived and trained.

The Riskers were a group of towering men and women, young and old, who never noticed her when she walked by. Not only did she walk among them, but she walked among dragons and had to be careful to avoid their tails and dragon droppings. Zora watched a young boy strain with a wide shovel to scoop up a huge dropping left on the street and shuffle away. She envisioned Grey Cloak and Dyphestive doing such chores when they were younger. *No wonder they left. Where is he?*

So far as she was concerned, she'd served everyone she could think of except the Doom Riders. No one even spoke about them, which was odd, because Dark Mountain's people were talkative. *I'm starting to think that they aren't even here. The obvious usually explains it.*

She was carrying uniform tunics on hangers that were draped over her arms. It was the second trip to Risker's Roost in three weeks, and she'd been tasked with embroidering new insignias on them. She hustled on foot to the commander barracks. A peg was next to a door that had a dragon painted it. Brass dragon gargoyles hung from the sides of the door. They had eyes that burned with green gemstones that gave them a realistic look.

Zora lifted the tunics and hung them on the peg. She never went inside or knocked, always doing as she was told. As far as she knew, no one was inside. She'd never seen or met any of them. Deeann always told her to "Do your business, avert your eyes, and move on."

As Zora turned to leave, a group of Riskers was marching by in full armor. She kept her head down but lifted her eyes their way. They were a young, fearsome bunch, full of brash talking. A blonde was leading the way, strutting with his chin up and chest out. He caught her looking and gave her a snide look. She looked away.

The door to the commander barracks opened suddenly behind her. She jumped forward a step and took a quick look back. Her heart jumped, and she tore her gaze away from the woman that glanced her way. *Drysis!*

There was no mistaking the one-eyed woman who had killed her friends. Drysis was as tall as any man and had ghost-white hair that was braided and fell over her shoulders. She was still wearing the dragon-scale armor of a Doom Rider.

Zora felt the woman's eyes boring into her back. She crouched down and started to walk away.

"You there," Drysis said in her commanding voice that

could hammer a nail in a wall. "Are you with the tailor shop?"

Subtly brushing her hair over her eyes, Zora turned. She kept her head down and nodded. "Yes."

"Come with me," Drysis said.

"As you wish."

Drysis marched down the road, out of Risker's Roost, and Zora followed quietly, walking like she was on pins and needles. She had no idea if Drysis would recognize her or not. They'd only crossed paths once in the streets of Raven Cliff, and that had been from a distance. Still, she wasn't about to take any chances. She covered up the best she could by keeping her head down and walking with a subtle hitch in her step.

"Are you a cripple?" Drysis asked. She walked with a very quick and long stride.

"No, your lordship. I dropped a—"

"I didn't ask what happened, did I?"

"Apologies," Zora said quietly.

Outside of the entrance to the camp of Risker's Roost was a separate path away from the main road that led downward. Zora had never noticed it because the road dead-ended at the camp's entrance. The long walk took them down the steep decline to where another smaller camp was nestled in the rocks. It had a small multilevel barracks and a barn behind it. A rock wall circled the entire camp. It was late in the day, and a firepit had been set up outside with a pig roasting on a spit over it.

Three huge men dressed in dragon-scale armor were gathered around the fire. They were the Doom Riders that Talon had battled before. Their heavy stares followed Drysis and Zora coming down the path.

A man with ugly scars on his face stood up and asked, "What's going on?"

"The monarchs are having a banquet for the Riskers, and I'm invited," Drysis said. "Not that it's any of your business, Scar."

"We don't get to go?" Scar asked.

"Of course not."

Scar flicked something into the fire. "We can't sit at this camp forever."

She shot him an icy look. "We'll have a mission soon enough. Besides, it's better than being dead, isn't it?"

The brawny warrior sat back down on the rock.

Drysis entered the barracks, and Zora waited at the threshold, facing the entrance. Deeann had taught her to never enter someone's establishment without being invited. She kept her back to the men too. *Please don't recognize me.*

A small rock hit her in the back of the head. She didn't turn.

"Say, what is your name?" Scar asked.

She didn't reply.

Another rock hit her in the back of the head. "What is your name, girl?"

Turning her head slightly, she said, "Zora."

"That's a pretty name. An enticing name. I like it. Why don't you come over here so we can get to know you, Zora?"

The men chuckled. Her fingers twitched at her side.

"You're making the little woman nervous," another man said.

"Stifle it, Shamrok." Scar walked over to Zora and leaned against the doorframe. With his finger, he lifted her chin. She tried to keep it down, but he was too strong. She kept her eyes averted.

"Look at me, pretty thing," he said.

Her chin trembled.

Scar sniffed her hair and touched the tip of her ear, and his voice deepened. "Part elf. I like it. I said look at me."

"Why?" she asked with a shaky voice.

"Because I think I've seen you before."

50

Zora squeezed her eyes shut. If Scar recognized her, they would kill her. *I'm dead.*

Drysis's strong hand reeled Zora into the barracks, and she punched Scar in the shoulder.

"Ow! Ettin's Ears, I'm only having some fun!" Scar said as he rubbed his shoulder. "I was just telling the little thing that I saw her in my dreams. Didn't hurt anyone."

"Go away," Drysis said.

Zora caught Scar sticking his tongue out at the commanding woman as she closed them inside. She chuckled silently. For some reason, the ugly man made her laugh.

Drysis shoved her down the hallway of the barrack and said, "Wait here." The warrior woman headed up the stairwell.

The woman's footsteps echoed as she walked on the floor above her, moving away. Zora leaned back against the wall and took a long breath. Her back was as tight as a bowstring. The mere presence of Drysis made her head ache.

Chopping noises came down the hallway, and the smell of freshly cut onions carried to her nose. She looked up at the ceiling. Not hearing any footsteps, she slid down the hall and took a peek inside the galley at the end.

A man was standing over a butcher's block, dicing vegetables and placing them in a bowl. His messy hair hung over his eyes as he bent over the table. His thick arms were covered in scrapes, bumps, and bruises, and his ragged clothing was filthy. *Poor fella. He must hate working here with these miserable people.* She glanced down the hallway and looked back. *I wonder if he's seen Dyphestive.*

The worker in the kitchen was staring right at her. His warm blue eyes were unmistakable.

Dyphestive!

Dyphestive looked away when she caught him staring. He went back to chopping the vegetables.

Zora couldn't believe her eyes. He'd grown some, but he looked absolutely awful. And the sorrow in his eyes melted her heart. He had the look of a broken man. *He didn't recognize me, but he's alive!*

Finding Dyphestive had been the plan. Contacting him hadn't. She had everything that she needed to report back to Talon, but the sad look on Dyphestive's big face got to her. She had to tell him something. She *had* to.

When she crept into the room, Dyphestive looked at her out of the corner of his eye but kept working. Using his knife, he scraped vegetables off the table and into the bowl.

Zora pulled her hair back over her eyes, stood beside him, and said, "Dyphestive. It's me. It's Zora."

He looked down at her. His face was expressionless and hard. All of a sudden, his blue eyes started to water, and he flung his arms around her and held her fast. He spoke quietly into her ear. "What are you doing here?"

The sound of Drysis's footsteps moved along the ceiling.

"Looking for you," she said quickly as she clasped his hand. "We had to make sure that you were alive."

"We who?"

"Us. You know, Grey Cloak... Talon."

His face brightened. "Grey Cloak's alive?"

She covered his mouth. "Shh! Yes. Listen to me. We have to figure out how to get you out of here now that we know you are alive. But it will take months. You have to wait. You have to be patient." She pulled away. Drysis's footsteps were at the top of the steps. "I must go."

"Wait." He grabbed her wrist. "We'll leave at some point on a mission. They are training me to be one of them."

"What?" She shook her head. "We can't worry about

that now. Do what they say in the meantime. Act normal. Talon will be watching." She rose on tiptoe and kissed his cheek. "Be ready, Dyphestive," she said. "Be ready."

EPILOGUE

For the next several weeks, Dyphestive went about his business with the Doom Riders with his chin up. Even though they did everything in their power to make him miserable, he handled it with a wellspring of hope inside.

Grey Cloak was alive. It was almost as good as him being alive himself. He didn't know how his blood brother had survived, but Zora's words had rung true. He believed her. The time had come for him to prepare himself for when Talon could save him. It was time to turn the tables and use his training for his benefit. When they came, he would be ready.

It was early morning, and Dyphestive was in the barn, feeding the gourn. They ate anything, alive or dead, like pigs. He carried a slain pig over his shoulder and tossed it over a gourn's stable gate. The gourn devoured the pig viciously. Hard bone crunched in the dragon horse's jaws.

Dyphestive cringed. He hated the grinding and chomping sounds. Then he headed for the livestock pen to slaughter another pig. The Brothers of Destruction preferred that he fed the pigs to the gourn live, but he hated the ear-splitting squealing. Besides, it was early, and he didn't want to wake anyone if he could avoid it.

When he was about to step outside, he saw Scar coming from the back entrance of the barracks. *Horseshoes!* He and Scar had been butting heads a lot more lately. Dyphestive's confidence was growing, and Scar didn't like it one bit.

"Boy, I need you to shoe my gourn," Scar said.

"What? This early? But I haven't fed—"

Scar whopped him upside the head. "Do it!"

Dyphestive lumbered back into the barn. The gourn had horse hooves on the back and leonine paws on the front. Only recently had he learned to not only shoe them but also saddle them and ride them. They were big mounts, seven in all, each in its own stall. They always looked like they were going to eat you.

"Which one?" Dyphestive asked.

"What do you mean, 'which one?'" Scar asked. "The same one I always ride."

Scar's gourn was an ornery beast with a disposition as bad as the man who rode it. Dyphestive opened the gate of the ugly scaled thing and stepped inside. He took the gourn by one of the lower horns that stuck out of its chin. "Come on," he said calmly.

The gourn sensed fear. If they didn't respect you, they would kill you. Luckily for Dyphestive, he'd cared for dragons much bigger than gourn before. He didn't fear them.

Scar closed the stable gate.

Dyphestive shot him a look. "What are you doing?"

"It's another lesson for you, boy. Let's see if you can take my gourn or not." Scar stuck his hand through the gate's bars. Something like tobacco was in his hands. The gourn sniffed it and reared. It roared, and its front paws clawed the air. "Calm him down, boy. Calm him down!"

Dyphestive pressed his body back against the stable wall. The gourn started to buck like a bronco. "Are you mad? Let me out of here!" he shouted.

Scar had climbed up on the stable gate and had an evil grin on his face. "You can handle it, boy! Take control and grab those horns! If I can do it, you can!"

Dyphestive watched the beast jump. The oversize stables were big but not big enough for the two of them. There wouldn't be any calming the gourn down, either. It had gone wild. Dyphestive made a break for the gate and tried to climb out.

"Get back in there, boy!" Scar shoved him inside.

The gourn flipped around at that exact moment. Dyphestive covered his head with his arms. The gourn kicked straight backward, and one of its powerful hooves kicked him in the skull. Dyphestive's body went numb, and the world went black.

"SCAR, WHAT HAVE YOU DONE?" Drysis shouted. She stormed into the barn with Shamrok and Ghost.

"There was an accident," Scar said. The gourn had calmed down, and he had dragged Dyphestive's limp body out of the stable. "The gourn kicked him square in the melon. I think the boy's dead."

Drysis kneeled beside Dyphestive and put her fingers on his neck. His head had a nasty gash across the top. "You'd better hope he's not dead, for your sake."

Scar shrugged. "What did I do? The boy was in the stable, trying to shoe my gourn. I told him not to do it that way, that he'd spook the beast. You know how stubborn he is, so I let it be. Sure enough, I turn my back, and the gourn goes buck wild. The boy's head snapped back like the crack of a whip. I think I heard his spine snap."

"You said Dyphestive was shoeing the gourn," Shamrok said as he looked into the stable. "Funny, but I don't see any shoes or a hammer."

In his mocking tone, Scar said, "I was on my way to get them."

If looks could kill, Drysis's boiling stare would have

killed Scar on the spot. Through clenched teeth, she said, "Fortunately for you, he's still breathing."

"He might be breathing," Shamrok said, "but he won't be doing much thinking. Not after that kick."

"Uh…" Dyphestive moaned. His eyelids fluttered open, and he took a deep breath.

Drysis sat him up, to the astonishment of Scar, whose eyes widened.

With a shaky hand, Dyphestive rubbed his head and said, "What happened?"

"Ha! He speaks," Shamrok said. He slapped Scar on the shoulder. "I can't wait to hear his side of the story."

Scar's jaw clenched.

"Do you remember what happened?" Drysis asked coolly.

Dyphestive shook his head. "My head's cloudy. Not sure."

Her eyebrows lifted. "Do I look familiar to you?"

"Yes," Dyphestive looked around. "But what do I call you?"

"Drysis." She pointed at Scar. "Who is that?"

"He looks familiar."

"Yeah, it's hard to forget ugly," Shamrok said.

"And them?" She pointed at Ghost and Shamrok.

"I'm not sure."

She smiled at him. "What about *your* name?"

Still wincing, he said, "That's easy, it's... it's... uh, I don't know. My head hurts too much."

"Do you remember what you were doing last?"

"Nope."

"But you recognize this place."

He turned at the waist. "It's the gourn barn. Right?"

She nodded. "Do you remember how you came to be with us?"

"Not really."

"But you recognize this place?"

He shrugged and pointed out of the barn. "Mostly. That's the barracks where I sleep, I think. What is my name again?"

"Help him up," she said.

Shamrok and Ghost assisted Dyphestive to his feet.

She hooked her arm in his and faced him toward the Doom Riders. "I am your commander, Drysis. These are your brothers, Shamrok, Ghost, and Scar. Sound familiar?"

Dyphestive nodded. "Yes, but who am I?"

Drysis cupped his face in her hands and said, "You, my child, are Iron Bones."

Is Dyphestive lost to the cause of the Doom Riders forever?

Will Anya survive her life-threatening wound?

PLEASE, leave a review on Sky Riders - Book 3. LINK. They are a huge help!

THE SAGA CONTINUES in *Iron Bones*: Dragon Wars – Book 4. On sale now! LINK Keep turning the page for more exciting details about this series!

And if you haven't already, signup for my newsletter and grab 3 FREE books including the Dragon Wars Prequel.

WWW.DRAGONWARSBOOKS.COM

TEACHERS AND STUDENTS, if you would like to order paperback copies for you library or classroom, email craig@thedarkslayer.com to receive a special discount.

GEAR UP in this Dragon Wars body armor enchanted with a +2 Coolness factor/+4 at Gaming Conventions. Sizes range from halfling (Small) to Ogre (XXL). LINK . www.society6.com

ABOUT THE AUTHOR

Craig Halloran resides with his family outside his hometown of Charleston, West Virginia. When he isn't entertaining mankind, he is seeking adventure, working out, or watching sports. To learn more about him, go to www.thedarkslayer.com.

Please leave a review. They are a huge help to me! LINK to Book 3.

*Check me out on Bookbub and follow: HalloranOnBookBub

*I'd love it if you would subscribe to my mailing list: www.craighalloran.com

*On Facebook, you can find me at The Darkslayer Report or Craig Halloran.

*Twitter, Twitter, Twitter. I am there too: www.twitter.com/CraigHalloran

*And of course, you can always email me at craig@thedarkslayer.com

See my book lists below!

Wrath of the Royals (Book 1)

Blades in the Night (Book 2)

Underling Revenge (Book 3)

Danger and the Druid (Book 4)

Outrage in the Outlands (Book 5)

Chaos at the Castle (Book 6)

Box set 1-3

Box set 4-6

Omnibus 1-6

The Darkslayer: Bish and Bone, Series 2 (10-book series)

Bish and Bone (Book 1)

Black Blood (Book 2)

Red Death (Book 3)

Lethal Liaisons (Book 4)

Torment and Terror (Book 5)

Brigands and Badlands (Book 6)

War in the Wasteland (Book 7)

Slaughter in the Streets (Book 8)

Hunt of the Beast (Book 9)

The Battle for Bone (Book 10)

Box set 1-5

Box set 6-10

Bish and Bone Omnibus (Books 1-10)

<u>**CLASH OF HEROES: Nath Dragon meets The Darkslayer mini series**</u>

Book 1

Book 2

<u>Book 3</u>

<u>The Henchmen Chronicles</u>

The King's Henchmen

The King's Assassin

The King's Prisoner

The King's Conjurer

The King's Enemies

The King's Spies

<u>The Gamma Earth Cycle</u>

Escape from the Dominion

Flight from the Dominion

Prison of the Dominion

<u>The Supernatural Bounty Hunter Files (10-book series)</u>

Smoke Rising: Book 1

I Smell Smoke: Book 2

Where There's Smoke: Book 3

Smoke on the Water: Book 4

Smoke and Mirrors: Book 5

Up in Smoke: Book 6

Smoke Signals: Book 7

Holy Smoke: Book 8

Smoke Happens: Book 9

Smoke Out: Book 10

Box set 1-5

Box set 6-10

Collector's Edition 1-10

Zombie Impact Series

Zombie Day Care: Book 1

Zombie Rehab: Book 2

Zombie Warfare: Book 3

Box set: Books 1-3

OTHER WORKS & NOVELLAS

The Red Citadel and the Sorcerer's Power